Penstock Canyon

The Mason Braithwaite Paranormal
Mystery Series, book 7

In this series:

Signs Point to Yes

The Desert Rats

Reach for the Sky

Billy Blood

Rubber-Band Ball

The Invisible Arrow

Penstock Canyon

The Man from Grapalia

The Mythical Blond

Stealth Glasses

The Melted Pineapple

Night on the Water

The Landers Mystique

Praise for the series:

Every foray by Church's wonderful psychic detective Mason Braithwaite is a truly suspenseful page-turner in the most unusual crime series ever, and certainly one that no aficionado of crime fiction should miss.
—David Osborn, author of the best-selling thrillers *The French Decision* and *Love and Treason*

Mason is a hero like none who have come before him: a sensitive, queer P.I. whose only weapon is his intuition. This book turns the detective genre on its head and makes you think about the ninety percent of your brain you're not using.
—Teja Watson, author of *Attic.doc*

Another fast-paced ride through Los Angeles by Church, who continues to reinvent and reinvigorate Mason Braithwaite. Church's writing is vivid, the worlds he creates believable, and his characters have a breadth of humanity, strength, and vulnerability that makes the series a fun-filled, page-turning adventure.
—Jeremy Randolph, author of *The Mural*

Thanks to Christopher Church for giving us another exciting and well written adventure with one of my new heroes.
—Amos Lassen

Penstock Canyon

Penstock Canyon

Christopher Church

DAGMAR MIURA

LOS ANGELES

Published by Dagmar Miura
Los Angeles
www.dagmarmiura.com

Penstock Canyon

First published 2018

ISBN: 978-1-942267-50-8

ONE

Pink chairs, a retro fountain that looked like a flying saucer, neat lawns and succulents, all wedged between towering office buildings—Grand Park was a cozy little space, modern and welcoming. Mason pulled one of the pink chairs to a shady spot, watching the toddlers and their parents play in the fountain. The renovated space—reclaimed from its former life as a parking garage—was perfect for Los Angeles, he thought, so often sunny, even though his red-headed complexion wasn't built for this climate.

Sipping on the espresso he'd bought on the way over, he scanned the pedestrians for Gilbert, who'd summoned him here for a meeting. Gilbert was a friend, and he often dropped in on Mason and his boyfriend, Ned, at their house, so Mason was perplexed as to why he wanted to meet downtown. But it wasn't really out of the way, and he could think of worse places to be on an early winter afternoon.

Gilbert was more Ned's friend than his, but they had built a rapport after Mason worked a case for him out in the desert, investigating an artifact found among his father's belongings. Ned accepted Gilbert's eccentricities unconditionally, but Mason still had trouble trusting him and his wide-eyed belief in any conspiracy theory he came across.

Soon Gilbert appeared, trotting down the stairs from the Music Center in oversize sunglasses, his unruly black hair bouncing with each step. Mason waved at him, and Gilbert nodded in acknowledgment but walked past him, into the coffeehouse and then out the back door, doing a circuit of the fountain and furtively glancing at the people lounging and playing in the water. Finally he approached Mason, pulling a pink chair into the shade with him and positioning it so he had a wide view of the public space.

"Good to see you," Mason said, pulling off his sunglasses and squinting at Gilbert. "You seem distracted."

"Have you spoken to Harmony lately?" Gilbert asked.

"No—what's going on?"

"She dumped me."

"Oh, Gilbert, I'm so sorry. Did she say why?"

"She said she couldn't see a future for us." He

scoffed. "I told her to talk to our mutual psychic friend, that you could tell her about the future, but she wanted to leave you out of it."

"It's probably just as well. I don't really do that. How are you feeling, are you OK?"

"I'll live. It was fun while it lasted, and it lasted longer than I expected. So I can't be too upset." He turned toward Mason, his eyes hidden behind his dark glasses.

Mason nodded, not sure what to say.

"Did you know she's not really Jamaican? Her legal name isn't even Harmony, it's Debbie or Stacy or something. Anyone can thread yellow and green beads into their dreads. It doesn't make you Jamaican."

"I wondered about that. But LA is a place people come to reinvent themselves, right?"

Gilbert sighed and folded his arms, scanning the park.

"Is there a reason for the big glasses?" Mason asked.

"I'm trying to lay low," he said, but pulled them off anyway.

Mason assessed him. "You look like you've been through the wringer."

"What are you talking about?"

"You look tired, and your eyes are bloodshot. The breakup must have been hard on you."

"It's not that," Gilbert said. "I've got bigger issues. It's why I wanted you to meet me here—my place might be bugged, and I thought the white noise from the fountain would cover our conversation if I'm being surveilled."

"OK," Mason said neutrally, looking him over again. Had he gone beyond the loopy conspiracy stuff to full-on clinical paranoia? "Who might be surveilling you?"

"My late-night visitors," Gilbert said. "I'm not getting any sleep. You helped me last time, in the desert, and this is kind of your field, the paranormal—can I hire you to look into it?"

Mason had never taken Gilbert's reports of late-night abductions seriously, filing them along with his other outlandish ideas: that Dutch elm disease had been created in a corporate lab to enrich tree nurseries; that the crowned heads of Europe were gradually being replaced by robots. But he was a friend, and he owed him the courtesy of listening.

"What happens, exactly?" Mason asked.

"They knock me out, so I'm not sure. Snatches of memory bubble up, sometimes in dreams—the big eyes. I have body memories of being frozen in bed at night, then floating, and being taken somewhere. I also remember animals that aren't really animals."

"What kind of animals?"

Gilbert looked away and rubbed his eyes. "A coyote sitting on my roof, looking at me. It makes no sense. Coyotes avoid people, and why would it be on my roof? Also an owl, standing in the street beside my car, looking at me with its big yellow eyes."

"That doesn't sound all that strange," Mason said.

"Except that it's four feet tall," Gilbert said

emphatically. "When's the last time you saw an owl like that? It doesn't exist. It was a screen memory, planted in my mind to mask what it really was."

"That does sound frightening. What do you think I can do to help?"

"I don't know, man," Gilbert said, irritated. "Whatever it is you do. Conjure something at the library. It's stressing me out."

"I get it," Mason said, eyeing him, surprised how quickly his anger had flared. "Let me do some reading, and I'll come up with some ideas."

"Great," Gilbert said, calmer now.

"Are you able to sleep in the daytime? Maybe you should crash when your visitors aren't around."

"Yeah, maybe I'll try that. It's dark in my place. I have all the windows blacked out." He stood and put his sunglasses back on, and when Mason rose, gave him a brief hug. "Talk soon," he said, and walked off.

Mason watched him trot up the stairs, then downed the last of his coffee and headed the other direction, toward the metro. He wasn't completely convinced what Gilbert was describing was really happening, but whatever the case, the guy was a wreck, and he wanted to help.

▪-▪-▪

Minutes later he climbed up the stairs out of the metro station in his neighborhood and found his bicycle, locked where he'd left it. The shadows were lengthening as dusk approached, but it was just a few minutes' ride home. The last block was up a hill and always got him panting. He put his wheels in the garage and went into the house. The sun just touched the horizon of their hilly neighborhood, on glorious display outside the French doors and beyond the balcony.

In the kitchen, behind the counter that separated it from the living room, he found Ned, wearing his apron and busy with a knife. He had dark Latin features, like Gilbert, but was infinitely more polished. Even chopping vegetables, he looked effortlessly well groomed, his shirt as crisp as if it had just been ironed. It hadn't, Mason knew; it was just the way his body moved, lean and lithe. Mason found it incomprehensible. No matter how hard he tried, most days he was a rumpled mess before he'd had lunch. Mason was tall and broad, and being disheveled seemed to go with it.

"Are you making dinner?" he asked, leaning across the counter and kissing Ned hello.

"Carrot soup and a couple of batards. How does that sound?"

"Amazing. Do you need any help?"

Ned grinned and shook his head. Mason usually skated on kitchen work, as Ned and their roommate, Peggy, were both enthusiastic vegan cooks.

"So what's up with Gilbert?" Ned asked.

"I'll tell you at dinner. I want to make some notes first." He went down the hall to their shared office and sat at his desk, switching on his banker's lamp and pulling a yellow notepad out of the desk drawer. He wrote down what he and Gilbert had talked about, then reread it, tore off the pages, and put it in a new manila folder. On the tab he wrote GILBERT'S VISITATIONS, then slid it into a drawer.

Soon after, he heard Peggy arrive home.

"Long day?" Mason asked, coming out of the office to greet her.

"I'm exhausted," she said, kicking off her conservative pumps and pulling the clip out of her long brown hair, letting it spill down her back.

"Hey, at least it's Friday," he said.

"Carrot soup and batards," Ned called from the kitchen. "It's almost ready."

"Let me change, and I'll come help," she said, her tone brightening.

Mason put utensils and napkins on the table, and Peggy soon returned, transformed from a gray law office drone back into herself, her wiry frame now comfy in sweatpants and a T-shirt. She whipped up a vinaigrette for the greens while Ned plated the soup and sliced the batards. Taking in the spread, Mason grinned and sat down with them, well aware that he was a lucky man.

"Gilbert asked me to work for him today," he said. "We had a clandestine meeting in Grand Park."

"What's his damage?" Peggy asked, tearing a slice of bread in half and dipping it in her soup.

"It has to do with aliens. I'm not saying I don't believe him, but we met in the park because he thinks his place might be bugged. He's looking pretty haggard."

"That's worrying," Ned said. "He's always been a little paranoid, but it sounds like it's getting worse."

"Harmony dumped him, so I think that might be an aggravating factor," Mason said. "I should probably take that as a sign that I should quit playing matchmaker."

"They're both grown-ups," Ned said. "What did he say about the aliens?"

"He's having memories of their big eyes, and he thinks they're abducting him in his sleep."

"It sounds like he might need a psychiatrist more than a psychic detective," Peggy said. "What does he want you to do, exactly?"

"He didn't really know. I'm going to read up on abductions and try to figure out what he can do."

"It's just so hard to believe," Ned said, tearing a slice of bread. "I've known him since we were kids, but this is really out there."

"I wish you'd cut me that much slack with my psychic stuff," Mason said, frowning.

"I do," Ned said emphatically. "I'm skeptical of both of you."

"Whether it's objectively true or not, it's real to Gilbert," Peggy said. "You may have to set aside your own beliefs." She turned to Mason. "While you're at it, you can assess whether he needs the mental-health kind of help."

"That's a great idea," Ned said. "If you think he's deluded, I can broach it with him."

"I'll see what I can find out," Mason said, and dug into his greens.

Ned cleared his throat. "Some other news. I've decided to buy this house."

"Whoa," Mason said, setting down his fork.

"Seriously? How did that happen?" Peggy asked.

"Well, I know how to get a mortgage, since I work with them all day. I bugged the owner about it, and eventually he agreed. I set up a private sale, just me and him and the bankers."

"Why am I only hearing about it now?" Mason demanded.

"I wasn't sure it was going to happen, but today I am."

"You're moving up in the world," Peggy said.

"A mortgage payment will be way more than rent, so I'll have less disposable income, which is in some ways a move downward. But I have a good feeling about it."

"Does this mean I'll be paying rent to you now?" Mason asked.

"Yes, and no discounts for sexual favors."

"I thought that was the deal you had with the landlord," he said, frowning. "It seems unfair not to maintain that tradition."

Peggy laughed. "That better not be true. He has a wife."

"The other option," Ned said, glancing at Mason and then looking down at his empty soup bowl, absently stirring the dregs with his spoon, "is to go in on the mortgage with me."

"But I'm not fiscally stable enough, am I?" Mason said. "I never know where my next job is coming from."

"You always make rent," Ned said. "There seems to be no end of people in this town who need psychic investigations."

"True," Mason said, "but it's a big commitment."

"It's more than just the house," Peggy said gently. "It would also be a commitment to your relationship."

"Good point," Ned said, setting his spoon on the table. "Of course, you don't have to decide now. Consider it, at least, and think about whether you want that. Don't think about the money, maybe, but just whether you're ready for it in other ways."

After he helped clean up, Mason stretched out on the sofa with his laptop. He couldn't even begin to think about money and mortgages right now—aliens seemed a lot more manageable. Looking for info, he quickly realized there was an overwhelming amount of material. The breadth of the subject was astonishing, with thousands of people claiming to have had alien encounters. Gradually he found that the research fell into two broad camps: those who thought flying saucers were mechanical ships from other planets, their occupants a biological species like our own; and those who thought it was a paranormal phenomenon, transcending the accepted rules of physics. That seemed more believable to Mason, closer to his own understanding of how the world worked, but Gilbert's description of his experiences fit more with the nuts-and-bolts theories.

He searched for material on owls and coyotes

and found that, along with wolves, they were the most common screen memories, placed there to disguise the true nature of the entity encountered. "Remember the eyes," one experiencer had written. "If you focus on the eyes, you can get to the truth of the memory." He made a note of that on his yellow pad; maybe it would be helpful for Gilbert.

Eventually he burned out on digging through the boundless information, and folded his laptop shut, closing his eyes for a minute. The library and its curated sources might be more productive, and there were people he could ask for advice. Several writers had also mentioned hypnosis as a way to access buried abduction memories, and Mason had actually used hypnosis once before. If Gilbert was willing, maybe he'd try it.

He crawled into bed with Ned, who was reading a novel. He set the book down when Mason climbed in beside him.

"I'm glad Gilbert asked for your help," Ned said.

"I hope there's something I can do. He seems desperate."

"He trusts you. I'm sure just taking him seriously will help."

One of the psychic tools Mason used to acquire information was lucid dreaming: he came to awareness inside a dream and could manipulate it. Tonight, however, he was only able to observe passively as it unfolded around him. He was in a park, or maybe a garden. Streaks of movement flashed in his peripheral vision, darting through the foliage, and each time he turned in that direction it was gone before he could focus on it. Once or twice he caught sight of a shape, just for a moment. He couldn't quite figure out what it was, but it looked like a tiny person.

▪-▪-▪

Sleeping until his body told him to get up always put Mason in a better mood than waking to an alarm. It was almost ten when he woke—technically still mid-morning, he told himself. Ned was out running errands and Peggy was gone too, so he enjoyed a quiet breakfast of fruit and a couple of pots of espresso before pulling on his backpack and heading down to the metro by bicycle. He took his bike with him on the metro, and was soon locking it up outside the central library.

It was an inspiring place to work—parts of it historic and elegant, others airy and modern—and Mason soon found an open desk near the stacks with books on flying saucers and the abduction phenomenon. Hanging his backpack on the chair, he pulled out his yellow pad and pen. First he dug into several books about saucer crashes, scanning what seemed superfluous and reading the key parts more closely. If every case were taken at face value, a dozen or more extraterrestrial spacecraft had come down across the country and abroad, most frequently in the desert Southwest. Then, many claimed, the military quickly swooped in, cleaning up the debris and threatening witnesses into silence.

He closed one of the volumes, *Crash at Corona,* and sat back to think. It was so hard to believe that any organization as inept as the federal government had pulled off a massive decades-long cover-up, and the books contradicted each other in some of the details. Maybe, like so many unsubstantiated stories, it wasn't all true, but part of it was true. Some of these accounts presented compelling evidence.

He wondered if part of his hesitation came from the fact that he didn't really trust Gilbert. His tendency was to discount anything the guy said, because so many of the things he said were outlandish.

He pulled another series of books, about abductions, and started reading. Not everyone considered the phenomenon to be negative, he learned; some writers used the term *contact* and said that they went willingly. Some experiencers found deep meaning and inspiration in it, afterward changing their lives for the better. A subset argued that that the whole thing was a religious experience, orchestrated by angels or demons, but those theories felt simplistic and were easy to discount.

He made several pages of notes, and after a few hours of reading he was convinced that something real was happening to these people. By extension, he knew he had to take Gilbert at his word. Despite the varying explanations, there were a lot of individuals going through the same experience, and the counterarguments—principally, that a large chunk of the population was deluded in exactly the same way—weren't convincing.

He stacked the books in a corner of the desk and read through his notes. "An observer can sometimes stop an abduction just by observing," he'd written. It came from one of the darker texts, *Abductions and Planetary Realignment: The Terrifying Plan for Planet Earth,* but it gave him an idea—he would watch Gilbert being taken from his bed at night.

Packing up, he walked out to the street, bleary-eyed but happy to be formulating a plan. The only problem he could see in it was how to stop himself from being switched off or frozen, like so many of the experiencers were—or worse, how to avoid being taken along with Gilbert.

Standing on the sidewalk, blinking in the bright light, he pulled out his phone and dialed Anna, a psychic he'd worked with before. She ran a seedy Koreatown storefront where she read palms and tarot cards, but she had years of experience in the field and had been a good resource for him. She soon answered, her idiosyncratic Eastern European accent unmistakable.

"Psychic center—how may I direct your call?"

He smiled at that; she usually worked alone, and her little shop didn't have room for more than a couple of people.

"It's Mason," he said. "Can I drop by your shop today? I might have a client for you."

"I have a couple of appointments in the evening, but come any time before then."

After stopping for an espresso, he went back into the metro, and before long he was in the glow of her front window, PALM READING spelled out in neon, arresting even in broad daylight. He locked his bike to a street sign and stepped in, a little bell jangling. He stood in the narrow room for a moment before Anna pulled aside the dark curtain blocking the doorway.

"Come on back," she said, pronouncing it *"byeck,"* a broad grin on her face, and he pushed his way through the dusty folds into a dim consultation room, a dramatically spotlighted crystal ball perched in the middle of the black-draped table. She led him through another curtained doorway into her cramped office, with a desk and a couple of folding chairs.

"Caffeine?" she asked, pouring herself a mug from the grubby carafe of an ancient battered coffeemaker.

"Sure," he said, and she poured another.

He took the cup from her, waiting to sit until she did.

"You have a client for me," she said, sipping her coffee.

"A woman who wants some tarot work contacted me through my Web ad, but I think you're more qualified to do what she needs. Do you have a pen?"

She found a pad of paper in the clutter on her desk, and Mason pulled out his phone, finding the message and then writing out the details.

"Thanks," she said, glancing at the note. "But surely that's not the only reason you drove over here."

"Cycled," Mason said, grinning. "And yes, I wanted to ask your advice. Do you know anything about observing something paranormal without getting caught up in it?"

"I'm not sure. What kind of paranormal?"

"Alien abductions."

Her eyebrows rose. "Well, now. That's a big one. I know this much: you don't want to get involved. It'll start happening to you too."

"See, I really want to avoid that," he said, meeting her eye. "A friend of mine says he's being abducted, and he's a complete mess. Have you worked with any abductees?"

"Not directly, but I hear things."

"Some people say it's technological, and some say it's completely paranormal."

She nodded. "What do you think?"

"I'm not sure. My friend's experience sounds mostly technological, but that might just be his interpretation of it, his own filters."

"I know a good way to get insight for paranormal incidents that involve technology," she said, leaning closer. "You watch channel 58."

"Is that a television network?"

"It's an empty channel on the old analog TV sets. TVs today just show a black screen when nothing is being broadcast, but the old TVs show static. You need to watch channel 58 on an old TV."

"What's on channel 58?"

"Nothing from this world. It's called the Pythic channel, and it's a conduit to deeper realms."

"So I just watch the static? For how long?"

"As long as it takes. You'll see static at first, but you'll get much more out of it than that." She tapped her temple knowingly.

"I guess I could try it," he said. He'd never heard of it, and made a mental note of the channel number.

"You should. You'll be surprised."

He drained his coffee, trying not to wince visibly at the bits of grit at the bottom, hoping they were just coffee grounds. Standing up, he set the mug beside the little sink.

"How's business?" he asked.

"You know how it goes—it waxes and wanes." She grinned. "It's hard to predict."

"Funny," Mason said, considering her business was predicting the future, and waved good-bye as he pushed through the curtains and back out to the street.

There was another psychic he could consult, a dabbler rather than a full-time businessperson, who nonetheless had decent skills and might have some ideas. He unlocked his bike and mounted it, then texted Peggy's boyfriend, Matt.

Hey man—time for coffee today?

He had just started pedaling down the sidewalk when the reply came.

Any time before 7. The place with the gravel patio?
Call me when you get here.

Matt lived downtown, in the Arts District, a century-old warehouse zone that had recently been overtaken with upscale housing and trendy eateries. Mason rode the rails most of the way, and texted Matt again after he locked up his bike. It was too chilly to sit outside, so he got a table inside near the windows and ordered a double espresso.

Matt appeared just as his coffee did. He stopped the waiter and asked for a soy latte. His brown hair was getting shaggy and he wore a few days' stubble, but in academia that was almost de rigueur. Matt was a living testament to the human capacity to embrace contradictions: even though he dabbled with paranormal phenomena, he taught hard science for a living.

"Yo, *cholo*," he said as he sat down. "Is this a social call, or are you here to extract information?"

"It's always a pleasure to see you, but I do have a work thing to talk about." He swirled the dark liquid in his little cup. "How do I observe a paranormal phenomenon without getting caught up in it?"

"What kind of phenomenon?"

"Alien abduction," Mason said, raising his eyebrows.

"Fuck me—seriously?"

Mason nodded.

"What do you mean, getting caught up in it?"

"I want to watch an abduction without getting abducted myself, or getting switched off."

"Switched off?"

"That apparently tends to happen to bystanders. They get knocked out—no memories, no dreams."

"I don't know anything about that, but I guess if you're going to fuck with aliens, there are a couple of things you could do."

"So you accept that they're real?"

"Why not? It's no more insane than half the things we've done."

"Agreed," Mason said, nodding.

"Do you know how to plug into power points?"

"What are those?"

"I'm not exactly sure, but the idea is that metaphysical energy is stronger in specific places. You can use your extrasensory perception to detect those points. Find the strongest one around, connect with it, and *bam*—you're supercharged. It might give you enough presence of mind to resist them."

"How do you find the power points?"

"Scope out the room, or wherever you are, using your inner senses. Then ask yourself where the energy is concentrated," he said, thanking the waiter as he set down his latte. "I have an idea of where there's one here. See if you can find it."

"Give me a second," Mason said, and Matt nodded, pulling out his phone and turning to the side, giving Mason some space.

Mason closed his eyes and cleared his mind, working to quiet the random thoughts that came up, tuning out the clatter of dinnerware and the conversations in the room. He thought about the kind of energy Matt had described, and expanded his consciousness outward. He didn't know exactly how he knew, as he didn't detect any direct inspiration, but in a few minutes he had a sense of several points in the room, and one that was definitely the strongest.

"I think I found it," he said finally, opening his eyes. He nodded to the window. "The table out there with the dog. It's about four feet over their heads."

"Right on," Matt said gleefully. "That's exactly what I got. If you found the same thing, there's definitely something to it."

"So how do I tap into it?"

"Focus on the point, draw its energy to you, and empower yourself. You'll feel it happening—it's unmistakable. I wouldn't do it now, though."

"Why not?"

"Because we're having a conversation here."

Mason laughed. "Got it. Thanks for the idea."

"There's another thing you can do that might work even better," Matt said. "It's a way to hide in plain sight. It's called cloaking."

"I think I've heard of that," Mason said, and sipped his espresso. The psychic craft had so many tangents—he'd seen the phrase in a book he'd read, or on a website, but not recently, and it hadn't come up in his research on abductions.

"I don't really know how to do it, but I can introduce you to someone who's pretty good at it. Gabriela Karma. She's an artist who works around here. I think it helps her when she's doing surreptitious street art."

Mason nodded. "I'd love to learn a new skill. Let's set up a meeting."

TWO

Wheeling his bike onto the train, he headed north to Lincoln Heights, where there was a thrift store the size of a small city. He locked his bike to the heavy iron fence out front, then went in and strolled through the racks of clothing, the familiar smell of aging fabric almost drawing him in for a quick look through the shirts. But he resisted, and continued to the room with the appliances, shelves packed with ancient kitchen technology, stereo speakers, cassette players.

Eventually he found what he was looking for: old-style TVs that were small enough to fit safely on the rack of his bike. There were a couple of options, but he picked the one with the scuffed and battered white housing, now a dingy yellow-green. The sticker on it read "$12," which seemed reasonable, so he picked it up and carried it to the register.

Catching the eye of one of the clerks, a woman in a denim shirt with close-cropped gray hair, he asked, "Can I plug this in somewhere?"

She pointed out a socket near the floor, and Mason spent a minute sitting cross-legged in front of the TV. He plugged in the cord, and it took a few seconds to warm up, but eventually the blue glow filled the screen, gradually coalescing into fuzzy static. He checked the labels on the controls to make sure it had 58, then twisted the dial, snapping through the channels. It looked as dead as every other channel, but at least it worked.

He pulled out the plug and stood up, then heaved the TV onto the counter, pulling his wad of cash out of his pocket.

"You didn't try it with a digital TV adapter," the clerk said. "You'll need one of those to watch anything. All the broadcast channels have gone digital."

"I don't need it to watch TV," he said, grinning as he counted out the bills.

She nodded and rang it up, handing him the receipt. "If you're planning to smash open the tube, be careful. Those things are loaded with lead and mercury."

"Thanks," he said, and lifted it off the counter. When he set it on his bicycle, it seemed bigger than it had inside, but with his bungees he was able to secure it to the rack. It looked odd, the gray screen facing backward, crisscrossed with colorful cords, but at least it wouldn't tumble off.

Back on the metro platform, there were already two bicyclists standing in the car with their wheels when his train pulled up. He considered waiting for the next train, but one of them waved him in, so he boarded and thanked them for making room.

"I didn't know they still made those," one of the riders said, eyeing the TV set. He was wearing bike shorts and looked extremely fit, and unlike Mason's bicycle, his ride looked high-end.

"It's from a thrift store," Mason explained. "It's probably older than I am."

"You couldn't find a flat-screen? There must be cheap used ones."

"It's for research," Mason said.

"You're going to pull it apart?"

"I'm going to watch it."

"OK," the guy said dubiously. "I guess everybody has their crazy thing."

Mason didn't reply, but he felt his cheeks reddening. He looked away, ending the conversation. Maybe it was a little crazy, but he didn't need that pointed out by a spandex-clad stranger.

Riding up the hill toward home felt especially laborious with the extra weight, and he stopped once to make sure the TV was still secured. Ned was home when he got in, lounging on the sofa with his novel.

"What the hell is that?" he asked, looking up as Mason came in with his acquisition in hand.

"Good day to you too, sir," Mason said. "It's for work. I'll explain later."

He carried the TV into the office and set it on his desk, then changed out of his sweaty shirt. Back at the sofa he joined Ned, who lifted his feet to make room, then draped his legs across Mason's lap.

"How was your day?" he asked, rubbing Ned's feet through his socks.

Ned gave him an update, but soon brought the conversation back to his earlier question. "What possessed you to buy an ancient mini TV?" he said. "Or did you find it in a Dumpster?"

Mason laughed, and told him about talking to Anna, and her advice about channel 58.

Ned was quiet for a minute, clearly struggling not to say anything judgmental. "Will it put you in a trance?" he asked finally.

"It should just work as a conduit, like a crystal ball or a Ouija board."

"How long will you have to watch?"

"I have no idea, but I'll get started tonight. I'll know when I get the insights."

Ned nodded. "Do you know if Peggy will be here for dinner?"

"Matt said they were doing something, so I doubt it."

After they'd eaten, Ned headed out to an AA meeting, and Mason went into the office. He got the TV plugged in and warmed up, and made sure it was on channel 58. The room light was distracting, he decided, so he turned it off and went back to his chair, settling in and focusing on the blue glow.

Before long he found his mind pulling patterns out of the static, like watching clouds and seeing people and animals. Even though the static moved fast, changing every instant, he saw houses, cars, faces. Eventually the patterns blurred and his mind started to wander, free-associating through what he'd read about today. At one point he caught himself thinking about rats running around, their feet leaving tracks in a freshly tarred surface. He pushed the unpleasant image away and worked to return to clearer thinking. Maybe channel 58 really was inducing a trance state.

Ned stuck his head in the doorway. "How's it going?"

"I thought you were going to a meeting," Mason said, squinting and looking up at him.

"I did—three hours ago. Are you seriously that caught up in the static?" He stood beside Mason's chair, glancing at the screen and folding his arms.

"I guess so," Mason said, rubbing his eyes. "It's hypnotic."

"Maybe you should come to bed."

"Soon. I think I'm getting something, but it needs some time to coalesce."

After Ned had retired he unplugged the TV and took it out to the sofa, plugging it in at one end and getting comfortable at the other. The screen was farther away than it had been on his desk, but he could still focus on it in the dark room, the only other light coming from the glow of the city outside.

Soon, although it wasn't clear to his conscious mind that he was getting any specific information, he was definitely in an altered headspace. He could *feel* the static now, the blue glow encompassing him.

Suddenly Ned was by his side again, wearing his breakfast boxers and a T-shirt. The gray light of early morning was coming in through the windows, he realized. He'd been at this all night.

"Are you awake?" Ned asked gently.

"Sure I am." Mason looked up at him and had to blink repeatedly to get his eyes to focus.

"You seem spaced out," Ned said, concern in his voice. "Surely you slept a little?"

"I can't tell. I don't think so."

Ned knelt and gently put a hand on the side of Mason's head, peering into his eyes. "Too much TV," he said. "Your irises have gone rectangular."

"What? Really?"

"OK, the fact that you believed that? Definitely too much TV." He sat back on his heels. "I'm worried about your mental health. This seems completely crazy."

"It's just static," Mason mumbled, stretching his arms above his head and yawning.

"Did you get the insights you wanted?"

"Maybe, yeah," he said, but as his mind swam up to normal consciousness, he had no sense that he'd learned anything. Instead he had a migraine, his head buzzing at the frequency of the static, his vision fuzzy and diffuse.

"I'll make us some oatmeal," Ned said. "Maybe it's time to turn that thing off?"

"Good call," Mason said, but even after he'd pulled the plug from the wall, when he closed his eyes he could see the ghost of flickering blue-gray static.

They ate at the counter, the oatmeal distracting Mason from his headache.

"Are you going to your parents' place today?" Mason asked.

Ned nodded. "You're welcome to come—there'll be food."

"I think I should sleep. If you leave now, though, you can make it to mass."

Ned snorted. "My mother would love that," he said between bites. "It took her longer to come to terms with the nontheist thing than the gay thing."

"I wonder which was harder for them," Mason asked. "The fact that you shacked up with a man, or that you shacked up with an Anglo?"

"They don't have any problem with either one. They love you. Plus they've both worked with lots of uptight people in their jobs, so it's not exactly a foreign concept."

"I didn't say 'uptight.' I said 'Anglo.'"

"Right," Ned said, raising his eyebrows. He took Mason's empty bowl into the kitchen. "I'm not sure when I'll be back, but I'll text you if I'm staying for dinner."

Mason went into the bedroom, where he stripped off his clothes and crawled into bed. As he closed his eyes, his head felt like it was vibrating in every direction, like the static on channel 58. Even with his headache and the rattle in his skull, he was soon asleep.

▬-▬-▬

Later, the ringing of his phone on the nightstand woke him. Grabbing it, he saw it was midafternoon. He'd been asleep for hours.

"Hey, Matt," he answered groggily.

"You lazy fuck. Were you napping?" Matt demanded.

"No, no, just having a snack. I've got peanut butter on my palate."

"You lie," Matt said flatly. "Do you want to meet Gabriela Karma this evening? She's up for teaching us the cloaking technique."

"Sure," he said. "Text me the time and place."

Ending the call, he dragged himself out of bed, pulling on a pair of shorts and walking out to the living room. He sat on the sofa, feeling weak and disoriented, almost jet-lagged. His head felt better, at least, the headache having faded along with the image of the static.

Anna's channel 58 exercise hadn't been productive, he thought, looking at the dead screen, still sitting at the end of the sofa. Maybe he'd try the thing Matt taught him, to find an energy point here. At least he knew he could do that.

He sat back and closed his eyes, expanding his awareness outward, to the whole room. Nothing came to mind at first, just the visual memory of the shape of the room, the dining table, the kitchen beyond the counter. Gradually he felt some bright spots in the air, the walls, and the floor, but he wasn't sure if they were energy points or just random noise induced by the static on channel 58. A couple were brighter than others, and he had a sense of thin lines running vertically into them from below, then up through the ceiling. One point specifically drew his attention, at the wall just left of the front door, around eye level.

Looking at the wall, it revealed nothing to his regular senses. He closed his eyes again and willed his mind to be placid. Focusing on the energy point, he thought about connecting to it, then about drawing energy from it. There was a twinge of something, he thought, some warmth, a subtle infrared glow in the stillness of his mind. When he opened his eyes, the room seemed more vivid, the colors brighter and more saturated, like a photo run through a contrast filter. He was aware of a sound that hadn't been there before, a subsonic throbbing coming from somewhere outside, or below him in the earth.

He shook his head to disengage from the energy point, and the room returned to its previous state, washed out and bland by comparison. Still, he had to smile; it was a neat new skill to have, and with any luck it would help him with Gilbert's abductions.

If he was going to practice cloaking with Matt's

artist friend tonight, he should probably do some background research. He wanted nothing more than to take a nap on the sofa, but he pushed himself up and made an espresso, then went to the office to grab his computer, returning to the sofa to read.

The first thing he found was about techniques to avoid detection used by ninjas during the Edo Period. They were able to hide in plain sight by staying still until there was no one watching, then moving swiftly, stepping heel to toe to keep silent. Mason had never been stealthy, but he liked the idea that it was possible to be invisible using real-world tactics. Other tricks they used were throwing rocks to distract attention, and mimicking animals.

He stood up and tried the heel-toe stepping on the living room floor, surprised that it really was possible to walk without making any noise. But as fascinating as it was, he knew he would need more than stealth to deal with Gilbert's aliens.

On the coffee table his phone flickered to life: Ned inviting him to dinner with his family. He texted back,

> Can't—have a meeting out. But find out if your
> mom has any potato tamales, without saying I
> asked.

His reply came a few seconds later:

> Why would it matter if you asked for them? She'll
> be happy to send you some.

Mason thought for a minute before responding.

I figure I should at least show my face if I'm going
to ask her for food.

He found some leftovers in the fridge for dinner before getting dressed. Thinking about the
ninja techniques, he picked dark pants and a plain
gray sweater. With his height and shock of red hair,
clothing alone was unlikely to help him disappear,
but it might even things out a little. Cycling to the
train station and locking up his bicycle, he rode the
metro to Matt's neighborhood, emerging well after
twilight.

Matt was waiting when he walked up, hands
jammed in the pockets of his hoodie against the
cool of the evening. He'd picked a quiet street to
practice on, lined with brick warehouses rather
than storefronts. The delivery gates were shuttered and dark, even though they were all gallery
spaces or office conversions these days, the whole-
sale businesses long ago having moved to roomier
neighborhoods.

"It's cold as fuck," Matt said as he approached.
"Gabriela's on her way. She hit traffic."

"I thought she lived around here," Mason said.

"There's no way a working artist could afford to
live in the Arts District."

Mason hadn't seen many pedestrians on the walk
over from the station, but at the next corner several people appeared, many of whom wore dark
clothes. As he and Matt watched, more joined the

group, some of them with camera gear.

"Is there a nightclub around here?" Mason asked.

"No, and they don't look like they're going clubbing."

"What do you suppose they're doing?"

"Let's ask," Matt said, and strode down the block toward them.

Mason followed, and listened as Matt spoke to a woman with a heavy camera slung over her shoulder.

"What's up with the gathering?" he asked her, the authority of a teacher in his tone.

"We're photographers," she explained. "We get together sometimes, and hire a couple of models," she said, gesturing to a young woman in a short skirt.

"She must be freezing," Matt said, and thanked the photographer. Walking back up the block, he said to Mason, "We'll have to find somewhere quieter for our thing once Gabriela gets here."

"Maybe she's already here," Mason said, "but she's cloaked."

Matt chuckled. "Well, hopefully she'll reveal herself soon."

They chatted for a while, and before long a figure turned the corner and walked confidently toward them. She was wearing a long cloak with the hood over her head, but she pulled it back as she stepped up to them, giving Matt a brief kiss on the cheek. The cloak was an unusual garment but appropriate for the weather, and it fit with what the photographers were wearing.

"Gabriela Karma," she said, smiling at Mason. She had Asian features but wispy blond hair with pastel blue streaks dyed into it, and very pale skin, which struck Mason as odd; it was hard to avoid the sun in this part of the world.

"I'm Mason," he said, nodding in greeting.

"Sorry I'm late," she said. "Some knucklehead flipped a truck on the 110. It was a circus."

"These people are doing a photo thing," Matt said, and at that moment someone switched on a spotlight, illuminating the scantily clad model climbing on top of a car. The clicking of dozens of shutters began, the swarm of photographers moving around in the street, jockeying for the best vantage point.

"It'll be quieter a block or two from here," Gabriela said, and they followed her onto a side street.

"I understand you're an artist," Mason said, glancing at the blotches of color on her hands. "I take it you paint."

"I started out as a tagger," she said, eyeing him with a grin, "but I transitioned into murals. I have a couple around here. I'll show you."

There was a lot of public art in the neighborhood, Mason knew, not all of it sanctioned by property owners.

"So what do you know about cloaking?" she asked.

"Nothing. I tried to read about it, but didn't find much."

"Good," Matt said. "You won't have any preconceived biases."

"I did research some ninja techniques for hiding in plain sight. One of their things is keeping still until you're not being observed, then moving fluidly."

"Cloaking is like that," she said. "Are you a ninja?"

"Oh, hell no," Mason said. "That would be like calling myself an accountant because I do my own taxes. I just read a little about their capabilities."

"This is yours, Snort," Matt said, stopping in front of a shop's steel window shutter, painted with a riot of looping blue and yellow lines, like a close-up of a box of colorful rubber bands.

"Yeah," Gabriela said. "It's not my best work. Funny that the only time you can see it is when the shop is closed, which means it's usually too dark to get a good look."

"Snort?" Mason asked. The word was written in the bottom corner in bubble-shaped letters.

"That's my tagging handle."

"You mean your artist pseudonym," Matt said.

She laughed. "Right—that does sound more marketable." She glanced around and said, "You know, we can practice right here. There's no one around."

"Let's do it," Matt said.

"OK. You two walk up the block a ways. Wait half a minute or so before you look back. I'll show you what I can do."

Matt put his hand on Mason's shoulder, and they walked together, waiting wordlessly on the deserted street. When they turned around, Gabriela was gone. The mural on the shutter, the unadorned brick walls were the same, but she wasn't there. She must have ducked around the corner, Mason thought. But then she appeared, stepping out from the wall, her dark hood up and obscuring her face.

Mason blinked, not believing his eyes. There was nowhere for her to hide, yet she had been there all along.

"Fuck me," Matt said, clearly as startled as Mason was. "Could you see her before she moved?"

"No, man, I was looking at a blank wall."

"Were you in front of the painting?" Matt called to her, then to Mason, "Maybe it helped her hide because of all the loops and swirls."

"It's not about the art," she said, pulling her hood off and walking over to them. "Part of it is about not moving, and part of it is getting your mind into the right state."

"What state?" Mason asked.

"The mental part of it is called 'hidden mind,'" she said. "Your mind is the root of your existence, so hiding your mind hides everything."

"I know that it works," Matt said, "because I just saw it happen."

"It works best at night, of course, and it works better with an actual cloak." She waved her arms, expanding the fabric of the garment, and grinned at them. "In the hills it might be better to wear brown or tan, whatever blends in with the landscape."

"What about the mental part?" Mason asked.

"That seems to be the key."

She nodded. "To get into hidden mind, you disperse your consciousness away from your center."

"Is it like astral projection?" Matt asked. "You send your mind elsewhere?"

She shook her head. "When you change position like that, your mind is still concentrated. Hidden mind is about spreading it so thinly in space that you become invisible."

"How do you achieve that, exactly?" Mason asked, folding his arms.

"It takes a while to get there, but basically, you defocus. Picture your mind spreading out, like a cloud of smoke, still connected and functioning, but thinned out."

"I'm sure I could do that," Matt said.

"You have to stay still, of course. Then, when you start to move, everything snaps back into place and you become visible. I think that happens because your body needs your mind to be focused when it moves. Some people say they can move and still remain dispersed, but I've never been able to do that. Maybe it's like your ninjas—a more advanced level of the skill."

"Can we try it?" Matt asked.

"That's what we're here for," she said. "Mason, you first."

"OK," Mason said dubiously. "I'm not sure how quickly I can get into that frame of mind."

"We'll face the street and give you a few minutes," she said. "If we can still see you when we turn around, we can try again. How does that sound?"

"I'll give it a try." They turned away, talking quietly, and Mason went over to the mural. A few yards down was another shop's doorway, not recessed enough to hide in, but it was painted a color that almost matched his sweater. He walked over to it as quietly as he could, stepping like the ninjas, rolling his sneakered feet from heel to toe.

He tuned out the streetlights, the trash piling up in the gutter, the sedan parked across the street. It was hard to imagine dispersing his mind—and a little frightening, the idea of losing control of his consciousness—but he imagined it spreading out, and when he thought of a confined bubble of space around him, he could feel it start to happen. He visualized his mind as a cloud of smoke, the image Gabriela had used, each particle drifting outward but still connected. That made it less worrisome: everything was still cohesive, just expanded. His vision started to flatten out, draining of color and contrast. That pulled him out of the mindset for a few seconds, but he was able to drift back into it, accepting the visual effect, willing the expansion to happen.

It felt like the first moments awake in the morning, when his mind was still empty, before the business of the day flooded in. He saw Gabriela and Matt turn around. Matt was looking at the mural and the blank wall, his brow furrowed, but Gabriela saw him almost right away, the streetlight glinting in her eyes, a grin playing on her lips. But he had fooled Matt, at least, and that was something. He smiled at the thought, and felt his mind refocusing just from that small physical action. Matt looked toward him now, able to see him as the hidden mind state dissolved.

"Not bad," Gabriela said, walking over to him.

"You saw me right away," Mason said, stepping away from the wall.

"I didn't," Matt said. "You were gone, man. Bravo."

"I'm skilled in the technique," she said, "so I know what to look for."

"It was definitely an altered state of consciousness," Mason said. "I was aware of you two, but I was kind of spaced out."

"Literally," Gabriela said, raising her eyebrows. "You're predisposed to doing it successfully, I think, because of your other psychic work. It's a gestalt, all the skills we develop, and it makes the new ones easier to acquire." She turned to Matt. "Your turn."

"I'm on it," Matt said, moving toward the wall. "Look away, both of you. Nothing to see over here."

Mason stood with Gabriela in the street, their backs to Matt.

"So where do you live?" Mason asked quietly. "You said you came on the 110."

"In Hyde Park. There are still affordable studio spaces there, although that might change soon enough." She talked for a few minutes about her art, explaining how she made a living from it, then said, "Let's see if we can find him."

They both turned toward the wall, and Mason scanned the length of it, not seeing Matt.

Gabriela laughed. "Not bad," she murmured.

Finally Matt materialized near the mural, stepping away from the wall into view. The effect was the same as when Gabriela had done it—until that moment, he had been invisible.

"Brilliant," Mason said. "You disappeared."

"Yeah, baby," Matt said emphatically. "I'm going to start hiding in banks at closing time."

"Don't. You'll get caught," Gabriela said. "Although I appreciate your confidence."

"So how does it work?" Matt asked.

"I have no idea," she said. "I think part of it has to be an interaction with the observer, because I'm able to see through it when other people aren't. But the mechanism of it is beyond me."

"I think it'll help me," Mason said, "but I'll have to practice."

"I'm glad," she said. "Do you think you have enough of a start? I should get going."

"I appreciate the instruction," Mason said, and fished one of his business cards out of his pocket, handing it to her. "If I can ever return the favor, give me a call."

She glanced at it and tucked it into her pocket. "I will."

"Thanks for coming out," Matt said, and gave her a brief hug before she headed back up the block.

"I hope it'll be enough to fool your aliens," Matt said.

"I guess I'll find out," he said, and after saying good-bye, started on his way back to the metro.

The whole thing felt tenuous, he thought, sitting on the train and watching the concrete walls flash past, but maybe that was just because he wasn't good at it yet. He'd need to practice, getting comfortable with that scattered headspace, before he could use it in the real world.

▆▆▆▆▆

Ned was still with his family, even though it was getting late, and the house was quiet and dark when he got home. He toasted some bread and spread hummus on it, disappointed that his tamales hadn't arrived yet, and was sitting at the counter finishing off the second slice when Peggy got home.

"I heard you spent the evening with Matt," she said, pulling off her shoes.

"We had a lesson on cloaking," he said. "He's pretty good at it."

"Let me get changed, and you can tell me about it," she said, and went down the hall.

It was an opportunity to practice, he realized. He could try hidden mind sitting right where he was. Maybe the sofa was better, as Gabriela had implied that a comfortable position was important. He slid off the stool and looked around the room. Not the sofa—right here, under the counter, he decided, beside the barstool, facing the living room. He'd be plainly visible to anyone who walked through the room, in the dim lighting, but he wouldn't be in an expected place.

He got comfortable sitting cross-legged on the floor and worked for a few minutes to induce hidden mind. It was harder now, because he felt the time pressure, to get there before Peggy came back. He cleared his thoughts and gradually was able to disperse his consciousness like a cloud of smoke. He felt the color drain from the room. It seemed like a long time before Peggy came back, even though it couldn't have been more than a few minutes. She walked into the room and hesitated, looking around, then stepped into the kitchen.

"Mason?" she called, walking past him again, just a few feet away, a blur in his peripheral vision. She went down the hall and called his name again in his bedroom, then came back, opening the French doors to look for him outside, even though it was a cold night.

"Where the hell did you go?" she said under her breath, closing the doors again.

Mason got to his feet, feeling his awareness instantly snap back into focus.

Peggy looked startled. "Where were you?"

"I was right here. You couldn't see me. I'm starting to think it really works."

She put her hands on her hips. "What are you talking about? And why are you grinning like an idiot?"

He sat in an easy chair. "It's what Matt and I were doing. Cloaking. I was able to disappear."

"Or maybe you were just hiding behind a chair in

a dimly lit room," she said, dropping onto the sofa.

"You walked right past me. I think I was invisible to your conscious mind."

She folded her arms. "Maybe. It is hard to believe that I wouldn't notice you there. You're a big dude."

"It's a psychic skill," he said, and told her about Gabriela Karma and learning the technique.

"What does she look like?" Peggy asked.

"Uh … maybe thirty-five, blond, and she has a moon tan. She was nice."

"Was she pretty?"

"I guess, for a woman. I can't really tell."

She laughed. "Do not try to sell me that one. You know damn well whether someone is attractive, regardless of their gender."

"Are you jealous?" he asked, a smile spreading across his face.

"Not in the least," she said, and looked away, but he saw that she was blushing.

"I don't think you need to worry about her and Matt. She left before I did."

"Good," she said emphatically.

"So what were you up to today? I thought you might come to learn about cloaking."

"Thanks, but I'll leave the psychic stuff to the psychics. I was cooking up a performance with my friend Lamar."

"I've heard you talk about him," he said.

Lamar was a choreographer, Mason knew, but worked as a security guard to pay the bills, much like Peggy worked for lawyers even though her true passion was music. For years she had performed her unique brand of folk music at small bars and coffeehouses around town, dressed as her stage persona, Peggy Pregnant, in flower-child garb and a maternity blouse over a massive fake baby bump.

"He got permission from one of his clients to do a pop-up performance in an abandoned hospital. We can bring people in to watch as long as we don't charge admission. We're doing it Friday night."

"Wow, that's soon. Will you have time to rehearse?"

"I'm already ready. My part of it is small compared to the dancers."

"Is he planning the choreography around Peggy Pregnant?" Mason asked.

"Her thing will kind of overlap with the dance performance, but they won't be dancing to my music. It's hard to explain. You'll just have to come and see."

"I wouldn't miss it."

▬▬▬

Mason was already in bed when Ned got home.

"You're awake," Ned said, coming into the bedroom and pulling off his shirt.

"How's the family?"

"Great. Mom sent you tamales."

"Sorry I couldn't join you. I had a meeting, and I was pretty wiped out from watching static."

"That's probably the single craziest thing I've seen you do," Ned said, climbing in under the covers and curling up beside him.

"I didn't really get much from it. I guess I need to be more selective about my techniques."

Ned chuckled. "That, I can get behind."

In the dream state Mason found himself floating in the limitless void, feeling his mind slowly dispersing. It wasn't frightening, and he didn't lose focus, but he could see each minute particle of himself, like dust floating in sharp light. Slowly he lost track of it, and the image collapsed into a jumble of static.

THREE

till burned out and weary from channel 58, Mason let himself sleep until he woke up naturally, and was startled to see it was well after eleven. He had a sandwich with Ned, then dropped an apple into his backpack and headed down the hill on his bicycle. He locked it up at the station and took the metro downtown.

He'd read a lot about saucers and alien contact in general, but he wanted to find out about interacting with the abductors. Returning to the shelves he'd been in on Saturday, he pulled out several books that sounded relevant, then settled in and flipped to a clean page in his notepad.

Contact experiences involved all sorts of beings,

he learned, scanning and reading through the sources, occasionally making notes. Some authors didn't think the abductors were even extraterrestrial, and some suspected they were actually intelligent machines. Some alleged that the military was complicit or even fully responsible, or that the government overall was clueless about what was happening to so many people late at night.

Experiencers described aliens that looked like blue dwarves, pale Scandinavians, and reptiles, among many others, including the classic grays. One writer had been abducted by something that looked like a canister vacuum cleaner, with a glowing eye mounted at the end of its metal hose. Even the grays came in several varieties, tall and short, some with big eyes, some that seemed more like *Homo sapiens*. Gilbert's snatches of memory implied that he was dealing with the grays, but none of the sources had specific advice about how to interact with them.

Some authors evoked more credibility than others, and as the afternoon wore on he was able to set aside some of the accounts and theories. One of the more pessimistic sources, a woman who had been taken against her will repeatedly over many decades, explained that the most helpful technique she had learned was to stay calm. "If the abductee can maintain a sense of sangfroid," she explained, "the interactions are more routine and end sooner." The aliens were interested in strong emotional states, she said, and fear specifically fascinated them. He wrote that down on his notepad and drew a heavy box around it. The very idea of seeing an alien was terrifying, he thought, folding her book closed and rubbing his eyes. He was going to have to steel himself for it.

Sliding his notes into his backpack and stacking the books on a return cart, he made his way outside, dismayed that the long shadows of dusk were already stretching across the little park adjacent to the library. Sundown came early in winter, but it felt like he'd hardly seen daylight at all today. He pulled out his phone and sat on an empty bench, then dialed Gilbert.

"*Pronto,*" a deep voice answered.

"Gilbert?"

"Oh, hey, man. How are you?" Gilbert said, switching to his regular voice.

"Why are you answering the phone in Italian?"

"I didn't know who it was."

"You don't have my number in your phone?"

"I did, but I had to abandon all my accounts and start fresh."

"But you kept the same phone number?"

"It's complicated," he said impatiently. "What's going on?"

"Well, I've done a lot of research, and I have to say, I sympathize with what's happening to you. Abductions sound pretty awful."

"So you believe me," he said. "I wasn't sure you did."

"I don't think I did at first," Mason admitted.

"Do you have any solutions for me?"

"First I want to observe the phenomenon. If you have an inkling when they might visit, I'll come by your place."

"They're coming tonight," he said. "Sometimes I don't anticipate them, and sometimes I can feel it. Right now, I can say I know they're coming tonight."

"Wow, that's soon," Mason said. He hadn't even started psyching himself up for it.

"I'm sure it'll happen again, if you're not ready yet," Gilbert said.

Mason thought about it. "Let me come over later, and we'll talk."

"Great," Gilbert said, enthusiastic. Just the knowledge that he was being taken seriously seemed to have cheered him up.

Mason pulled his apple out of his bag and sat there munching on it, looking around the park, the last of the daylight fading, streetlamps taking over. This was as good a place as any to try the hidden mind technique—not too crowded, darkness falling, plenty of open space. He ditched the apple core in a trash bin and chose a spot atop a low wall with a lamppost, bordering the stairs leading up to the building's entrance. It wasn't an unusual place for someone to sit, but it was near the library patrons coming and going, and they would certainly notice him.

He got positioned with his back against the post and pulled his knees up, hands comfortably in his lap. Watching people walking into the library, every one of them glanced at him, some with a little smile if their eyes happened to meet. He closed his eyes for a minute to clear his mind, then opened them again as narrow slits, trying not to focus on anything. He thought about how Gabriela had explained the technique, and imagined his mind expanding again, all the microscopic bits billowing outward in a cloud, filling the air. His field of view seemed to soften and slow down, and gradually he drifted into the fuzzy trance of hidden mind.

In his peripheral vision a woman walked by, not looking at him. It could have just been urban indifference, but as he waited, three more people went into the library, all of them oblivious to Mason. Compared to the attention he'd gotten before he'd entered this state, it probably meant that it was working, that they weren't noticing him.

A young man carrying a skateboard walked up the side of the stairs and almost brushed into Mason, passing inches from his knees, oblivious to him. That was too close, Mason thought dreamily. They really weren't seeing him. A few more people went by, alone and in pairs, thoroughly ignoring him, and then an elderly woman, bundled up with a sweater and a heavy scarf against the cool of the evening, her wispy gray hair tightly pulled back, came slowly up the steps. She was looking right at him, he realized with a start, and he shifted his eyes to her. The movement brought him out of his altered state. She smiled at him, her eyes bright.

"Keep at it," she said. "You're doing well."

"Thanks," Mason muttered, feeling his cheeks reddening, and he slid off the wall as she walked inside. She'd spoken in Spanish, he realized, yet somehow he'd understood what she meant. Maybe his altered state of mind had been especially receptive, or more likely, she'd projected the ideas to him, parallel with the spoken words. What a gift. She must be a *bruja* or a *curandera*, a traditional healer.

Brushing the gritty dust off his butt and adjusting his backpack, he headed toward the metro station. It was embarrassing that the *bruja* had known what he was up to, but at least she'd been the only one of a dozen people who had actually seen him. He still didn't feel he was ready to face Gilbert's aliens, not completely, but at least he was developing a skill that might help.

Peggy had made a tempeh salad for dinner, with crunchy celery and scallions in a hearty mix that they ate with crackers and slices of bell peppers.

"So I'm going to Gilbert's tonight to talk about the abductions," Mason said after they'd sat down. "I think I've done all the research I can."

"How are you planning to help him?" Peggy asked.

"I'll hypnotize him and see where that leads. I'm also thinking I should try to observe the abduction."

"Interesting idea," Ned said, picking up a slice of

pepper. "I wonder why Gilbert never had his girl-friend do that?"

"If someone else is in the room, they just knock you out, and you don't remember anything. But I've learned a couple of techniques that might help me stay conscious."

"The best thing you can do for him," Peggy said, "is assess whether he needs medical help, or even just a counselor. Having someone to talk to can help a lot."

"I know all about that," Mason said, and smiled. He had a weekly appointment with his own shrink. "In my reading I've run across several people who specialize in counseling abductees, so it's on my radar."

Mason helped them clean up and then went to the bedroom to change. He donned dark pants and the same gray sweater he'd worn to meet Gabriela. It would blend into Gilbert's dingy apartment if he decided to use hidden mind. He looked himself over in the floor mirror. It could pass for stealthy, he decided, but still, the idea of watching Gilbert get abducted made his heart pound.

At his desk he pulled the pad out of his back-pack and tore off the notes he'd made today, reading through them to refresh his memory and then sliding them into the GILBERT'S VISITATIONS folder. He left his backpack under his desk and headed out, cycling down to the boulevard, his bicycle light feeble next to the glare of car headlights. He waited a while for the bus, which happily had space for his wheels on its front rack, and in minutes he was in Gilbert's neighborhood, cycling up the hilly side streets.

At the bottom of Gilbert's driveway, he locked his bike to a parking sign. The house looked completely abandoned. The ground-floor apartment had been empty for years, as the building was technically uninhabitable, having been yellow-tagged after an earthquake, but Gilbert somehow managed to occupy the upper floor. His windows were always dark, Mason knew, because he had completely covered them from the inside with metal foil to block radio waves. Gilbert had never been able to explain clearly who might be monitoring him through his windows or beaming waves in at him, but he seemed content living in perpetual darkness. He'd moved his kitchen table and chairs onto the roof so that he could enjoy the sun sometimes, and Mason had to admit the rooftop made a nice little outdoor space, shaded by trees farther up the hill and with a sweeping view of the neighborhood below.

The driveway was beyond the reach of the streetlights, and as he walked up, he pulled out his phone and turned on its light, holding it above his head to navigate. He followed the pool of illumination it cast, walking up the driveway, then up the stairs. There was no bell, he knew, and he pounded on the heavy steel-lined door with the side of his fist, hoping Gilbert would hear the dull thump from inside.

He did, soon pulling the door open and welcoming him in. No one would have guessed from looking at the place from outside, but the apartment was warm and well lit.

"Do you want some tamari almonds?" Gilbert asked, holding out a plastic bag from the bulk store. "I'm addicted to these things." He didn't seem as stressed out as he had in the park, or as tired.

Mason shook his head. "I just ate."

"Suit yourself." He dropped onto the ancient sofa, setting the bag of almonds on the coffee table in front of him. Mason sat across from him in the lone easy chair.

"So what have you learned?" Gilbert asked.

"A lot. So many people are going through the same thing as you. I'd like to try a couple of things, including watching it happen."

He frowned. "They'll just switch you off. That's what they did to Harmony when she was here. She'd wake up and have no memory of me getting taken."

"There are psychic techniques to resist that. I'd like to try it, at least. We can do it tonight if you're willing."

"Hell, yes. I'm at the end of my rope."

"Before that, I'd like to try to hypnotize you, and maybe pull out some clearer memories of what happens."

"I'm guess I'm up for that. Have you done it before?"

"Of course. It's a standard technique."

"What do I have to do?"

"Get comfortable," Mason said, "and listen to the sound of my voice."

"Done," he said, and lifted his feet onto the sofa, stretching out fully, folding his hands over his belly.

"Close your eyes," Mason said softly, leaning back in the chair. He'd actually only done this once before, but it had worked quite well, and Gilbert definitely seemed to be the suggestible type. "When you want to relax in nature, do you go to the mountains, the beach, or the desert?"

"I don't really do that," Gilbert said. "But if I had to, I guess I'd pick the beach."

"Good. Imagine walking along the shore," he said, trying to speak calmly and evenly. "You can hear the waves breaking, and feel the sand under your feet." He spoke for a few minutes, describing the sensory experience of the seashore. The goal was to shift Gilbert into a calmer state of mind, so he could dig into obscure memories in his subconscious. "When you open your eyes, you'll be calm and focused. Go ahead, open them."

Gilbert blinked a couple of times and stared at the ceiling.

"How do you feel?" Mason asked gently.

"Dude, I'm not under," he said, turning his head toward Mason. "What's with all the talk about the beach?"

"It was supposed to put you in a trance. I guess it didn't work."

Gilbert sat up. "Nope."

"You're not even a little relaxed?"

"Nothing's changed since you started talking,

although it was boring, so I almost drifted off. What's plan B?"

"I guess I'll watch you sleep. When do you usually go to bed?"

"Soon," he said. "Will you be in bed with me? I can change the sheets."

"No," Mason said quickly. He was never quite sure whether Gilbert was flirting with him or not, but no way was he climbing into his bed. "I want to be across the room, and awake."

"Let's figure it out, then," he said, rising and walking toward the back of the apartment. Mason followed him into the bedroom, which was surprisingly roomy.

"It smells good in here."

"Patchouli," Gilbert said sadly. "It's the ghost of Harmony."

"Sorry," he said, and stepped over to the headboard, which had three little compartments stuffed with books. "I didn't know you were a reader."

"You condescending ass," Gilbert said, putting his hands on his hips. "You think I'm illiterate? You saw my dad's house. I grew up surrounded by books."

Mason could feel his cheeks turning red. "I'm not trying to be rude. I just didn't know you were into books."

"I'm not. Not really," he said, smirking now. "I'm just messing with you. Those are Harmony's."

"Well, why don't you get rid of them, and spray some air freshener in here?" Mason said sharply.

"Or, god forbid, open a window? It might help you move on."

"Let's focus on the aliens," Gilbert said. "Where do you want to be while I'm sleeping?"

Mason looked around the room. "Maybe between the closet door and your dresser," he said. If he sat on the floor, he'd have a good view of the side of the bed from a safe distance away. He wasn't sure if the visitors would come through the door or not, but he'd be far enough from there too.

"We can move the dresser a little," Gilbert said, and they each took a side and shifted it a foot or so along the wall.

"Looks good," Mason said, sweeping away the newly revealed dust bunnies with his shoe. "I'll be comfortable here."

"I'll get you a pillow to sit on," Gilbert said, returning a minute later with a sofa cushion. He went into the bathroom to brush his teeth, and Mason settled onto the floor, getting as comfortable as possible. Gilbert came back and snapped off the room light, leaving just the glow of the little reading lamp on the headboard.

"Can you sleep with that on?" Mason asked. "It might be good to have some light in here."

"Sure," he said, and twisted the lamp so it was pointed up the wall, leaving the bed in near darkness. "Will that work?"

"I think so," Mason said. "My eyes will adjust."

Gilbert pulled back the covers and unself-consciously stripped off his clothes. Mason thought he should probably look away, but he didn't, and watched Gilbert's dimly lit naked silhouette climb into bed.

"If it gets uncomfortable on the floor, you're welcome to climb in and keep me warm," he said, his head propped up on one palm.

"Do you know how inappropriate that sounds? I'm in an exclusive relationship with your best friend."

"I'm not going to molest you, Mason. I'm just saying the bed is the most comfortable place in the room."

"Thanks, but we might have better luck if I keep an objective distance."

Gilbert chuckled and rolled over.

Mason spent a minute with his eyes closed, breathing evenly, clearing his mind. Once he was relaxed and had quelled the random noise of his thoughts, he focused on finding the energy points in the room. It took a while to expand his awareness and tune in to them. Eventually he found the one he wanted, undeniably the most powerful point, floating above Gilbert's headboard, almost at the ceiling. He imagined plugging his mind into it, being energized by it, the unseen power of the world flowing into him. He could feel it happening, the connection slowly forming, first as a feeling of warmth in his body, growing into a sense of keen awareness. He opened his eyes and found he could see better than before. Part of it was just his vision adjusting to the dark, but it was more than that, the saturated colors and the reading lamp brighter, its light filling the room.

The sound of Gilbert's breath became steady and even, and as Mason listened, sitting motionless, his breathing gradually grew deeper, and a mild snore developed, the air rattling in his throat. He smiled at how raspy it sounded. With that racket, he was in no danger of falling asleep himself.

Not knowing how long it would be until the visitors arrived, he decided to induce hidden mind now and try to sustain it. He shifted to get more comfortable against the wall, hoping he could maintain the position for a few hours without his legs falling asleep. Imagining his mind expanding, he worked to induce the altered state, spreading his consciousness in the space above his head. After a while he knew he was in the right headspace, but he willed himself to go deeper, remembering the connection to the energy point, and with each minute became more and more diffuse, more spaced out. He could still see the room and the bed in front of him, but it was hazy, like a dim copy of a copy superimposed on his field of view.

He sat that way for hours, it seemed, unmoving, his consciousness dispersed. *Stay hidden*, he told himself. *No matter what happens, stay hidden.*

He felt them coming before he saw them. The knowledge of what they were was terrifying, but it stayed buried, a flaming sphere of panic lodged down in his gut that he was aware of but that didn't overwhelm him. He hung on to the hidden mind, not shifting, not even moving his eyes as they materialized at the foot of Gilbert's bed. There were three of them, spindly and gray in the dim light, impossibly bulbous heads atop sticklike bodies. If he'd been in a clearer frame of mind he knew he would have screamed.

Two of them moved to the sides of Gilbert's bed, the third remaining at the foot. Its head turned slowly to survey the room, the blank black eyes looking toward him. He'd imagined encountering this creature, or robot, or whatever it was, and had seen numerous sketches and renderings, but none of it prepared him for facing one of them, standing here and staring at him. The roiling ball of terror in his gut pushed upward, wanting to break through his dispersed state of mind, but he ignored it and looked through the creature, ignoring it too, and after what seemed like an eternity, it turned away.

Gilbert floated up from the bed, horizontal and stiff as a board, levitating in midair without the entities even touching him. They stood watching him for what seemed like ages, unmoving. It was impossible to assess the passage of time in this state of mind; it could have been seconds, minutes. Then the four of them seemed to stretch upward, elongating or maybe blurring as they moved toward the ceiling for a moment, and then winked out of existence.

He waited, in case something else was going to happen, and because he knew that returning to regular consciousness would mean letting the suppressed terror explode and burn through him, but nothing changed, the dim glow of the reading lamp illuminating the wall, Gilbert's messy bedsheets in the shadows. Finally he willed himself to move, tilting his head forward and closing his eyes. Things didn't snap back instantly, the way they had before, but took a few seconds to fall into place. Panic surged, making his heart race, knotting his stomach, and he staggered to stand up. Sitting immobile for so many hours had switched off his muscles, and he stumbled, collapsing onto the side of the bed. *They're gone,* he told himself, willing his heart to slow down, breathing heavily to dispel the adrenaline.

Logically, though, they'd be back. Despite the success of cloaking himself from the visitors, his instinct, the primal urge, was to run—out the door, down the stairs, down the driveway, back to the safety of his own bed. He struggled to find rational thoughts beyond that, and ran his fingers through his hair, rubbing his head, to calm himself down.

They'd floated through the ceiling, which implied that wherever they were taking him was up there, maybe a ship hovering over the neighborhood. If he'd been able to conceal himself from them in here, surely he could do that outside, and maybe watch them come back. It wasn't any more risky than what he'd already done.

He stood and found his balance, still stiff from inactivity, and walked slowly into the living room, carefully stretching his arms and rotating his back. He pulled open Gilbert's refrigerator, wincing at the sudden bright light, and found a half-full bottle of lemonade in the door, along with half a dozen bottles of beer. He pulled out the lemonade and considered drinking out of the bottle, but Gilbert probably did that. He found a glass in a cabinet beside the sink and poured lemonade into it, gulping it at first and then savoring the tartness. It brought him into sharper awareness, better clarity. He realized that he'd been in hidden mind for so long that tendrils of it still curled around his consciousness, and he did a couple of neck rolls to try to dispel it completely.

Returning the bottle to the fridge and setting the glass in the sink, he went to the front door and heaved it open, stepping outside. He could see better now than when he'd arrived, his eyes attuned to the low light. It would be so easy to trot down those stairs and back to safety, but he didn't, resolutely turning the other way and walking up the stairs to the roof. Treading as silently as possible, using the ninja steps, he felt a surge of fear as he neared the top, but pushed it down, trying to stay rational.

Stepping onto the roof, he scanned the sky, but there were only a few dim stars visible in the glow of the city lights. The last time he'd been here, the flat roof had been empty save for Gilbert's kitchen table and four chairs, but now there were several potted plants, and a garden hose stretched out near them, snaking up from the back of the building. The table was in the middle of the roof, above the living room, and the potted plants were lined up toward the back, over one side of Gilbert's bedroom. Where could he watch from? He thought about leaning against the pots, but if they brought him back right above his bed, the plants were too close, just a few steps away. The most logical place for him to be was under the kitchen table, which also afforded a view of the top of the stairs.

He squatted and crawled in underneath it, shifting one of the chairs out of the way to get a better view and leaning against one of the table legs. The surface of the roof was meant to be waterproof, not inviting and loungeable, but he folded his legs and got as comfortable as he could, the top of his head almost touching the underside of the table, the gritty roofing material radiating dull cold into his bones. The open part of the roof above the bedroom was far enough away that he felt safe, and he focused his gaze on it, narrowing his eyes.

He didn't take the time to connect to the power point, but started the process of dropping into hidden mind. It came quickly, easily this time, drifting back into the state he'd been in for so much of the night. He could feel himself sinking deeper into it without willing it. Some part of him found it familiar, comfortable.

It didn't take long. The three stick beings appeared in a blur, almost like they'd dropped out of the air, right where he'd expected them, above the bedroom. The table blocked his view of the sky, and he wanted to look up, wanted to see where they'd come from. But he knew he couldn't move, couldn't leave the dreamy hidden state. Seeing them again brought the same sense of fear, raw terror at seeing something so utterly strange. He knew the panic was there, raging and burning just below his fragmented awareness, even though he was disconnected from it.

The beings were in the same configuration as when they'd left, Gilbert's naked body stretched out, floating and unmoving, in the middle of the trio. They stood on the roof for the briefest time before they blurred again and dropped through. Not long after, the three of them reappeared, minus Gilbert, stopping for a moment, then blurring upward and disappearing.

Mason waited a while before he moved, dreading the flood of emotion to come when he regained his regular state of mind. Eventually he did, first moving his hands and his knees, gulping air to catch his breath as if he'd just surfaced from a deep dive.

His heart was pounding but he wasn't completely back from his diffuse state when he spotted something moving in the periphery of his vision. It was behind one of the chairs, in the dimness at the top of the staircase, climbing over the low wall around the edge of the roof. It was a coyote, ears flat, slinking with its head close to the ground. That didn't make any sense; why would a coyote climb onto the roof? He shifted position to get a better look, and saw that it wasn't a coyote, but a man, crouching on all fours. He turned toward Mason, noticing him now that Mason had moved. He met his gaze and smiled.

"Don Luís?" Mason said. He'd come across this guy before, months ago, at a séance, the night he'd first met Matt. He knew he was a powerful psychic.

Don Luís spoke, a rapid string of Spanish syllables, only a few of which Mason understood: "*Mason* and "*Por qué.*"

Mason remembered that he didn't speak English. "*Lo siento,*" he said, struggling with the pronunciation. "*No comprendo.*"

Don Luís sighed and stood up, and Mason followed suit, awkwardly crawling out from under the table and getting to his feet. He was a full head taller than the elderly *brujo*. Don Luís spoke again, but this time Mason understood, as if the meaning were projected into his head. It was the same skill the woman outside the library had used, transcending the language gap.

"What are you doing here?"

Mason had no idea how to telepath the meaning of his own words, so he answered in English. "They took Gilbert. He's a friend of mine."

His eyes narrowed. At first Mason thought maybe he hadn't understood, but it wasn't that.

"You saw them, but they didn't see you?"

"I learned a technique," Mason said. "Hidden mind."

"You seem to have mastered it," he said. "I didn't see you at first either."

It was an odd sensation, hearing the words spoken in a language he couldn't speak and yet understanding them.

"What are you doing here?" Mason asked.

"Checking up on what these things are doing. I'm not brave enough to sit and watch them, but I can feel it when they come around."

"Do you know Gilbert?"

He shook his head. "You should get out of here. The *chaneques* are attracted to the energy these things use. Can you feel it? It's just peaking now."

"Not really," Mason said. "I don't understand the word *chaneques*, what is that?"

"Little people. Bogles. You don't want to mess with them."

"People keep telling me that," Mason said. "Thanks."

Don Luís walked back to the top of the stairs. "Go," he admonished him, before disappearing. Mason could hear his footfalls descending the metal steps, quick and confident for such an elderly man.

FOUR

ason looked around at the rooftop, lit only by the ambient light of the city. It seemed so ordinary now, although if he really thought about it, maybe he could feel the energy Don Luís had talked about. More than just cold, the air felt sharp, had an almost electric tang. It was odd that the *brujo* had just walked up here, and hadn't really explained why he'd come. Why would he be shadowing Gilbert's abductors?

Thinking about it, he was sure he had seen a coyote stepping onto the roof, not a person. Don Luís was a diminutive man, but he didn't look anything like a coyote. Mason had still been swimming up out of his altered headspace, still shocked from seeing Gilbert's abductors. His brain must have misinterpreted the input from his eyes, assuming he was seeing a coyote. But Gilbert had said he'd seen a coyote on the roof.

He sat down on one of Gilbert's kitchen chairs, exhausted and emotionally drained. Even more than tired, his head was still woolly, he realized, not completely back to normal, still slightly dispersed, still partly hidden.

Again there was movement at the top of the stairs, and Mason watched in shock as a little man stepped over the wall and hopped onto the roof. He was tiny, the size of a toddler, but unlike an ordinary person with a growth disorder, he had the proportions of a full-size adult. Three more of them climbed over, similar in stature. They were dark-skinned, like indigenous people, and were dressed in dark clothes. Like the photographers on the street in the Arts District, Mason thought, not even trying to think rationally. There had been so much strangeness tonight, and he still felt cognitively impaired.

They glanced at him one by one but seemed unconcerned by his presence, walking toward the part of the roof where Gilbert and his abductors had stood a few minutes earlier. One of them was female, he saw, and one of them was hopping rather than walking, part of one leg missing.

"He's got your haircut, Rudd," the little woman said as she walked by.

One of the little men did indeed have red hair,

noticeable even in the low light, but it looked like he never combed it. Mason hoped his own hair looked better than that.

"He's still got both feet, though," the redhead said, "so he's smarter than Rowan."

"What's *she* doing here?" the last one said, scowling and looking Mason up and down.

"I'm working," Mason said, irritated at the shade. "What are *you* doing here?"

Almost instantly he regretted opening his mouth, because the little one whirled around.

"Good gods," the redhead said. "He can see us."

The woman turned back, peering at Mason. "He's got second sight. Maybe from the visitors' energy. He must have been here the whole time. I wonder how they missed him."

Mason sat in silence, not sure whether to engage with them or just get up and leave. So far they weren't talking to him, just about him. They didn't seem intimidating, but these were the little people Don Luís had warned him about.

"Hey, person," the one they'd called Rudd said calmly. "Whatcha doin'?"

"You're the *chaneques*," Mason said.

The angry one, the one who had called him out, rocked from one foot to the other with palpable fury. "Should I kick his ass?"

"Back off, Sour Alan," the little woman said. And to Mason, "You're a special one, if you can see the visitors without them seeing you."

"I'm not intrinsically special. I just acquired

some psychic skills to avoid detection."

"Curious," Rudd said, watching him with sharp eyes.

"We call that second sight," the woman said. "I'm Heather, the leader of this band. This is Rudd," she said, gesturing to the redhead, "and Sour Alan, and the guy with one leg is Rowan."

"I'm Mason," he said. They stood watching him expectantly, so he added, "Pleased to meet you."

"Finally," Sour Alan said, and slapped his thigh.

Heather grinned. "Come with us to our camp. It's not far."

"Why?" Mason asked.

"I want to discuss those skills of yours. Maybe we can learn something. It won't take long."

"I wanted to go down and check on my friend."

"The one who got taken?" she asked. "It's happened before. He'll be fine. Let him sleep."

In his dazed state of mind Mason knew what was happening, that he was talking to four miniature people. He knew it was odd, but it didn't seem alarming. Maybe he could learn something from them too. "What the hell," he said, and got to his feet.

"Good," Heather said, sounding surprised that he was willing. "Follow us."

"Can't we stay a while?" Rudd said, looking longingly toward the back of the roof. "Maybe Gigantopithecus here can wait a few minutes."

"Can you hang on a sec, big guy?" Heather asked him, cocking her head to the side. "We'll be quick."

"Sure," Mason said. He sat on the kitchen chair again, dazed, and watched as they trooped over to the part of the roof where the abductors had stood with Gilbert. Rudd started hopping around, twirling, almost dancing, joyfully flailing his arms around. The others soon joined him, their movements ecstatic, like preschoolers hopped up on high-fructose corn syrup, or a cat in the thrall of catnip. He tried to tune in to what they were feeling, the energy Don Luís had mentioned. All he could sense was the crispness in the air.

After a few minutes of wild exertion they stopped, walking toward the stairs one after the other, panting and grinning.

"Come on," Heather said, waving for him to follow.

Mason got up and followed them down the stairs, past Gilbert's front door to the driveway below. They moved fast, considering how small they were. Rowan didn't let his disability slow him down, hopping along at the front of the group. They went single file into the trees behind Gilbert's house, and Mason had to stoop to follow them under the evergreen branches.

They should have emerged into the next yard, which Mason knew was there, just beyond the stand of foliage between the properties, but they were still walking among trees, and the hillside had flattened out. Completely disoriented, he looked around for streetlights, but there was nothing but the sky-lit woods. It made no sense. There was no parkland or green space anywhere near here, just streets and houses. Yet on they trudged through the woods, Mason hustling to keep up with Rudd, the last in the line. He knew this neighborhood, but somehow he was completely lost.

"None of this looks right," he said finally.

"Things look different at night," Heather called back to him. "We're almost there."

The woods ended suddenly, and Mason stopped short, startled as he stepped into open space, a grassy field surrounded by trees. At the edge of the woods stood eight or ten tepees, lit by a flickering fire at the center of the clearing. A gap in the ring of tepees revealed a patch of darkness—water, he realized, the inky blackness reflecting the stars above. No way was this anywhere near Gilbert's place.

The four walked toward the fire, climbing onto a circle of logs that surrounded it, and Mason followed. The fire was small but the logs were arranged close to it, and he felt its warmth.

"Sit with us," Heather said, perching on top of a log.

Mason stepped over the log and decided to sit on the ground, leaning back against it, so he wouldn't be towering over his hosts. Rudd sat nearby, but Rowan and Sour Alan chose to sit farther away, almost behind the fire. Rowan seemed to be happily watching the flames, but Sour Alan glared at Mason suspiciously. There were other little people here, he realized, glancing around and seeing movement at the flap of one of the tepees, a pair of eyes glinting in the darkness beside another.

"Your people are shy," he said.

"It's understandable," Heather said. "It's not very often that they can be seen by your people. Tell me how you acquired second sight."

"You mean why I can see you? I have no idea."

"How are you able to hide from the visitors?"

"It's a psychic technique," Mason said. He shifted position to get comfortable, then explained the hidden mind. Heather barraged him with questions about where he'd been, exactly, when he saw the visitors, how close they'd been, what they looked like, how he'd felt. He answered as clearly as he could, and eventually she seemed satisfied.

"So what do you know about them?" Mason asked. "The visitors."

She chuckled. "They smell amazing, don't they?"

"I saw your reaction, but they didn't really have that effect on me."

"I find that hard to believe," Rudd said. "They're irresistible."

"What are they?" Mason asked.

"I don't know," Heather said.

"We do have theories, though," Rudd said.

"Enlighten me," Mason said. "Please. I've read a lot, but I've found no answers."

"My, my," Rowan said, looking toward him from the other side of the fire. "He's so polite." He mimicked Mason's intonation: "Please."

Sour Alan cackled, but Heather ignored them. "Have you heard the idea that we're living in a simulation run by an advanced intelligence? The thinking goes that our entire universe might be simulated."

"I have heard about that," Mason said.

"We think the visitors might be envoys or avatars sent by the architects of the simulation. Why they would do that, I don't know, but there's evidence."

"Like what?"

"Well, they seem to be able to defy the established laws of physics, for one. It's one of their hallmarks. They can also manipulate time."

"I can do that," Mason said. "Slip backwards a little, at least."

"That's just changing positions," she said, meeting his eye. "The visitors can stop the flow of time in a specific location. No one of this world can do that."

Mason nodded, and looked into the fire, considering the idea.

"They sound like gods," he said finally.

"No," she said firmly. "Gods are created by people. The architects created the universe. They're just scientists running an experiment, as fallible as you and me."

"You sound like my boyfriend," Mason said. "He's not a fan of gods and demons."

Heather shrugged. "It's just a theory. I have no more information than your people do."

"Except that you can see them," Mason said. "And smell them, or enjoy their energy, whatever it was you were doing on my friend's roof. And they don't switch you off."

"I think they could if they wanted to," Rudd said. "But they seem much more interested in you people."

"Why do they take us?" Mason asked. "What do they want?"

"Who knows?" Heather said. "Maybe they're checking up on how things are progressing in their simulation. It's a mystery."

"I'll say," Mason said.

Heather sat up, her hands on her knees. "Rowan has a question for you, don't you, Rowan," she said, eyeing him.

"Right," he said. "I'll be right back." Mason watched him hop to a tepee on the other side of the fire, then return a minute later with something in his hands that was bigger than his head.

He hopped up and stood before Mason, who saw that it was a loaf of bread, disc-shaped and flat like a ciabatta. It must have just been baked, because it smelled amazing—better than Ned's, if that was even possible.

Rowan pulled the loaf apart, showing surprising strength. It split unevenly, into a small piece and a larger one.

"Which one would you like?" he asked, offering both to Mason.

The aroma was mesmerizing, and his instinct was to take the larger piece and sink his teeth into it. But he resisted the urge. "If we're all sharing it, just break me off a smaller piece," he said.

"Choose," Rowan demanded, raising his voice.

"Dude, chill," he said, and quickly took the smaller piece. It was still warm. Rather than biting into it, he looked around to see whether he'd be eating alone, whether he should wait.

"Ha!" Rowan shouted, tossing the rest of the loaf to Heather and dancing around the fire.

"You idiot," Sour Alan shouted, scowling at Mason.

"The green cap for you," Rowan crowed, and hopped off toward the tepee again, returning with a loop of green fabric. In a flash he leapt up on the log behind Mason and pulled it onto his head.

Heather and the others cheered, even Sour Alan managing an unenthusiastic "Huzzah."

Mason reached up to feel the hat. It was light, maybe cotton, but it had a soft peak on top that flopped forward, like a Phrygian cap.

"Don't take it off," Rowan shouted to him, waggling a finger.

"What's happening?" Mason asked, leaning toward Heather.

"Beer, that's what's happening," she said, nodding toward one of the tepees, where two new faces appeared, carrying metal tankards in each hand. Other little people had begun to appear as well, drifting toward the fire, abandoning their hiding spots. There were maybe twenty of them in all, young and old, some eyeing Mason curiously, but most focused on distributing the tankards. A smiling woman handed one to Mason, carrying it in both hands and struggling with its weight, as it was much larger than the others.

Heather said, "Cheers."

Mason popped the lid up with his thumb and took a cautious sip; it was a delicious light ale, yeasty and sweet, with a thick head.

"You're making a mistake," Sour Alan said, tankard in hand and foam on his upper lip, looking at Rowan, who ignored him. The others had joined them, sitting on the logs, chatting and drinking.

"Don't listen to him," Rudd said, catching Mason's eye and talking over the noise. "You chose wisely."

"Eat," Heather said, nodding at the hunk of bread in Mason's hand. She had torn a chunk off the larger piece and passed it down for the others to share. Each of the little people tore a bit off before passing it on, munching on the bread and drinking from their mugs.

Mason took a bite and felt overwhelmed. It was the best bread he'd ever tasted, crisp and chewy and perfect. Maybe it wasn't even bread, but something new, a heightened experience beyond mere bread. He savored every delicious bite, washing it down with the beer, and soon had polished it off.

One of the other *chaneques*, a woman with dark eyes and skin lined with age, approached him, nervously shifting her weight from one foot to the other. She looked him in the eye and asked gravely, "How do you get around your city?"

"Uh ... by bicycle," he said, meeting her gaze.

The woman guffawed, covering her mouth, then

clinked her tankard against Mason's.

"Is that funny?" he asked, but she only laughed harder, tears of mirth in her eyes, and stepped away.

A young-looking man came up from the other side, less timid than the woman but equally serious, and asked, "What do you eat for your dinner?"

"Nothing as good as your bread," he said. "I guess mostly vegetables."

This was also greeted with laughter, from the one who'd asked as well as others within earshot. Soon he was surrounded by a phalanx of faces, by turns serious and highly amused, one by one asking similarly inane questions: What was his favorite color? How many holes were there in his belt? Which shoe did he put on first? Every answer evoked great hilarity. It was confusing, but Mason went along with it, answering honestly and laughing with them, drinking when they clinked their tankards to his.

Rudd hung around until the questions had all been asked and the group had dispersed. He seemed interested in Mason in a different way, looking at him thoughtfully.

"Do you get a lot of grief for your red hair?" the little man asked.

"All the time," Mason said, happy to have something in common with him.

Rudd smiled. "I know how it is."

"How long have you been camped here?" Mason asked him.

"We've been here forever. Since time began."

Mason nodded. "Indigenous people always say

that when they don't have recorded history."

"Well, we've been here as long as anyone can remember, then," Rudd said, scowling. "That's a reasonable definition of 'forever.'"

"Fair enough," Mason said, and lifted his tankard toward him with a grin. He hadn't meant to cause offense.

"Time works differently for us anyway," Rudd said, mollified. "It makes it very difficult to keep track of what you people are doing."

"So why do you have English names if you're indigenous people?" Mason asked.

"That's about you, not about us," he said. "You hear English names because you speak English. We're not even really speaking English."

Mason frowned. "What?"

"This isn't what you think," Rudd said, gesturing vaguely. "Our names are Spanish when your people speak Spanish, and we have Tongva names that you couldn't even begin to pronounce."

Mason thought about that. In a way it made sense—Don Luís and the woman at the library had been able to talk to him without using language.

"It just seems like I'm hearing English," he said. "And it's the only language I speak."

"There's nothing objective about this experience," Rudd said. "You left that behind when you followed us into the woods."

"What are you talking about?"

"What do you see when you look at our houses?"

Mason glanced around at the pointed structures

looming beyond the fire. "I'd call them tepees," he said.

"That's because you think we're Native Americans, and you think Native Americans live in tepees," he said.

"Aren't you? Indigenous, I mean?"

"We are, but not in the way you think."

Mason looked at the tepees again, the flickering light of the fire illuminating the white fabric, poles protruding from the top. "If those aren't tepees, what the hell are they?"

"It's interesting that you called us *chaneques*. It reveals your filters, what your assumptions are. We're also called fairies, or brownies, depending on who you ask."

"I thought brownies were all wizened and ugly."

"Slander," Rudd cried, but then laughed.

"Shame," Sour Alan called out, his voice deep. He was sitting a few feet away, and must have been listening to their conversation.

Heather clapped her hands loudly a few times and said, "Drink up. All good things must come to an end."

Mason set down his tankard and prepared to stand.

"You didn't finish it," Rudd said, nodding to the tankard. "You have to drink it all."

"Seriously?" Mason said.

"You ate your bread, now drink your damn beer," he said, putting his hands on his hips.

Mason complied, draining the vessel, and then

said to Heather, "Thanks for your hospitality."

Most of the *chaneques* had drifted away, back into their tepees, a few faces watching from the safety of the interiors.

"You're obligated to us now," Heather said. "And what a coincidence—there's something you can do for us in your world."

"Slow down," Mason said, not standing but shifting position to face her. "I don't owe you anything."

"Yes, you do," she said firmly. "You drank our beer and ate our bread. In return, you'll do us a favor."

"I can pay you for the beer, if you'd like. I assumed it was honest hospitality."

Heather's face clouded. "Don't you go questioning my honesty. You're sitting there wearing the green cap, but you're acting like a boor." She stormed away to confer with Rowan on the other side of the fire.

"Keep calm," Rudd said, his voice barely audible. "No matter what happens."

Mason nodded, almost imperceptibly. It was worrying—the implication that he was somehow in peril.

"This has to be resolved smoothly," Rudd continued quietly. "Otherwise they'll take you back on the wrong path, and you'll find yourself in a time when you're younger than your grandchildren."

His heart pounded at the words. He remembered Don Luís's warning. Why hadn't he taken the elderly *brujo* seriously?

"Ask your reflection in the pond what to do."

Mason closed his eyes for a second and breathed deeply, telling himself to stay calm. Rudd's advice sounded absurd, but he'd presented it like a sage clue, and it was all he had to work with right now. He was a little tipsy, he realized, from the beer, and probably from being awake all night. When he opened his eyes, Rudd had moved away.

"Heather," he called.

She turned around and looked at him expectantly. "What?"

"I'd like to consult with my reflection about how to handle this."

She looked surprised, but said, "Of course you can do that. The rock should be big enough even for an oversize galoot like you."

She walked over toward the water, and Mason rose, absently dusting off his butt, and followed her. There was indeed a big rock at the waterside, flat and smooth.

"We'll leave you to it," she said, and stepped away. They were taking it seriously, he realized, all of them standing well back near the fire.

Mason knelt on the rock and put his hands on its edge, peering over into the blackness. He could just see his reflection in the still water, his hair sticking out around the floppy cap on his head; he'd forgotten he was wearing it. It seemed foolish, talking to his own reflection, but it wasn't that far out of line with the swirl of absurdities that he'd been caught up in this evening.

"Am I in danger here?" he said quietly, watching his own lips move. "What do I do?"

"You don't owe them anything," his reflection said.

He was so startled he almost lost his balance, pulling back before he tumbled into the water.

"Steady on, man," his reflection admonished. "Listen carefully. They're trying to play you. Make them pay you, like it's a job. It's not safe to refuse them outright, like Rudd said, but you don't have to work for a chunk of bread and some beer either."

"Damn," was all that Mason could manage. It was like watching a recording of himself.

"Tell them how it's going to go down, but keep your sangfroid."

He really was listening to himself. He'd just learned that word today at the library, reading a book that had used it. He'd had to look it up. It was fresh in his mind, and here he was, spouting it at himself.

"Look sharp," his reflection said impatiently, nodding toward the fire.

"Thanks," he said, and sat back. It was a lot to absorb, and he stood up slowly, thinking as quickly as he could. He went back to the fire, resuming his previous place on the ground, his hands passively in his lap. Heather stepped over and folded her arms, looking at him expectantly.

"So what is it that you'd like me to do?" he asked.

"We want you to stop one of your people from building a monstrous structure on land that's important to us."

"I don't work for free," Mason said. "I'll research

your property dispute, but I have to get paid."

Her face broke into a smile, and she unfolded her arms with a flourish, a coin appearing between her thumb and forefinger, seemingly out of thin air, like a magician's trick. She held it out to Mason. He took it from her, admiring it. It was lovely, lustrous gold, and oh-so-beautiful, shining in the firelight. He was captivated, and couldn't take his eyes off it, turning it over and over in his fingers. What a fascinating object.

"Nice, isn't it?" she said. "We'll pay you as many of those as you can fit in your pockets—if you can stop the construction." She reached out and gently pulled the coin from his hand.

He let it go, reluctantly, his eyes following it into her pocket, saddened to see it disappear. If he could just look at it for a little longer.

"Well?" she asked.

He sighed. "Deal. Where's your piece of land?"

Instead of answering, she spat into her right palm, then held it out to him. He hesitated, then reached for it, but she pulled her hand away.

"Spit on it, or it's not binding," she said.

He worked up some saliva and spat into his own hand, revolting as that was, then reached for hers, shaking it delicately, careful not to apply too much pressure. Her hand was the size of a baby's, and it felt warm, and disgustingly slimy. He resisted the urge to wipe his hand on his pants.

"Tell me about your construction project," he said.

"Rowan," she called over her shoulder. "Fill him in."

Rowan hopped over and sat on the log beside him. "The land is on the hill that's all alone by the sea."

"In LA?" he asked. "What neighborhood?"

"I'm not sure. It's nearby. Less than a day's walk."

"I don't really walk," he said, but he thought about the image, a lone hill near the water. "Maybe Palos Verdes?" he ventured.

"Part of the hill is covered with nodding donkeys."

"It's a farm?"

Rowan struggled to explain. "Nodding donkeys. They nod all day, all night. Endlessly."

"Oil pumps," Mason said, suddenly understanding. "I know where that is, the hill with the oil pumps." It wasn't near the ocean, not really, but it wasn't too far from it, and it certainly was a hill on its own, in the middle of South LA. But it was a big area, mostly unincorporated, as far as he knew, ringed with residential neighborhoods.

"The construction site is near the oil field?" he asked.

"The land faces the north star," he said. "Nothing rises higher, but much land falls below it."

"OK," Mason said, and thought about that. "So it's on the north side of the hill?"

"Perhaps," Rowan said, shrugging helplessly.

If that's where it was, it had to be either Blair Hills or Baldwin Hills. "Nothing rises higher" must mean it was near the top of the hill.

"Is there something on it now?"

"No—it's our land," Rowan said.

"So it's a forest, like this one?"

"A meadow. Close your eyes and imagine it."

Mason did, even though he had no inkling what he was supposed to envision, but that didn't matter—when he closed his eyes he could see the land, a complete image of it, long and shallow, rising toward the back, covered in dry grass and weeds. The clay bluffs of a hilltop towered in the distance.

"I can see what it looks like," he said, although he suspected Rowan knew that. "What's the construction planned for it?"

"A palace fit for a sultan."

"I guess that shouldn't surprise me, in this town," he said. "You know, I think I know where it is. Generally, at least. There can't be that many undeveloped parcels in that area, and I've seen it up close now. I should be able to find it."

"Good," Rowan said, sliding off the log and balancing on his lone leg. "We'll take you back, so you can get started."

"It might take some time," Mason said. "How can I contact you if I have questions?"

He laughed. "You don't. We'll contact you."

Before he could reply, Heather said impatiently, "Time to go," and clapped her hands three times. The others clapped thrice in response, even the ones lurking in the shadows. She looked at Mason. "Rowan will take you back."

Mason got to his feet. "Are you sure you're up for this?" he asked.

"I could outrun you on your silly bicycle," he said cheerfully. "Follow me." He hopped toward the brush at the edge of the woods.

"It was nice to meet you all," he said, looking around at the group, then followed Rowan.

Mason had to hurry to keep up with him, stepping over foliage and around tree trunks. Rowan used the forest to propel himself, swinging off branches, springing off logs, a graceful blur, his foot in the air more than on the ground. Before long they emerged onto Gilbert's driveway, his familiar sedan a reassuring sight.

"Do you know where you are?" Rowan asked. He didn't even sound winded, even though Mason was.

"I do."

"Give me the hat."

Mason pulled it off, handing it to him, and ran his fingers through his hair.

"Well, good-bye, then, seer," Rowan said with a grin, and hopped back into the brush.

Mason watched him disappear, then walked down the driveway. He considered going up to see Gilbert, but decided against it. As Heather had said, he was better off getting some sleep. They could talk tomorrow. He found his bicycle and unlocked it, looking back up the driveway. From here he could see the lights of the next house through the copse, just a few yards farther; it made no sense that the *chaneques* had been camped up there.

Climbing onto his wheels, he pedaled off toward the boulevard. There was little traffic, so he rode on the streets and the sidewalks. He wasn't buzzed anymore, he realized, feeling the cold night air on his face. He was hungry, too, despite the bread he'd eaten. Thinking about the *chaneques* and their camp, now that he was back in familiar surroundings, it all seemed patently unreal.

The house was dark when he got in, and Ned stayed sound asleep as he peeled off his clothes and crawled into bed. He checked the clock when he plugged in his phone, shocked to see it was only a little after three. He had been sure it was almost morning, and had expected to see dawn breaking on his way home, attributing its absence to the limited daylight of winter. Gilbert had gone to bed well after eleven, and he'd waited hours before the visitors came, and then Don Luís and the *chaneques*—the timing was way off. But he couldn't worry about it now, drifting into sleep, the random images and sounds of the hypnagogic state tumbling in his mind. Suddenly Heather's face appeared among the imagery, looming large.

"Don't forget," she said firmly. "You owe us."

FIVE

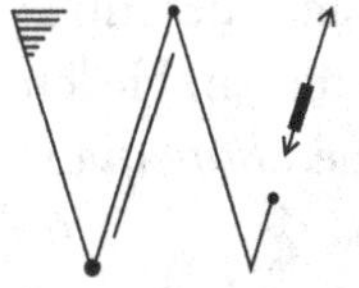

Waking when his body decided to, Mason lay in bed for a while, cozy and relaxed, appreciating the bright midday light outside the window, blissful in the drowsy beginnings of consciousness before his mind caught up to being awake. Inevitably it did, the events of the previous night crashing into his awareness like a garbage truck, memories of liminal beings made real. Aliens.

Lying there, he ran through it all. It felt so dreamlike in the details. But he knew it had really happened, remembered the suppressed terror at seeing Gilbert spirited away, Don Luís the coyote, shaking Heather's saliva-slimy doll hand. He heard the clatter of dishes in the kitchen, so he rolled out of bed, pulling on some clothes and stopping to wash his face.

"I didn't hear you come in last night," Ned said. "I made coffee. Do you want a sandwich?"

"Maybe fruit," Mason said, stifling a yawn. He was grateful for the hot java, which he poured into a mug. He washed a couple of apples and a ripe persimmon, then joined Ned to eat at the counter.

"So how did it go?" Ned asked, biting into his sandwich.

"Everything Gilbert told us was true. I saw them take him. They floated him right through the ceiling."

Ned's eyes grew wide. "Seriously? You saw the aliens?"

Mason related what he'd seen, and described moving up to the roof to watch them return. He left out the part about Don Luís and the *chaneques;* the abduction was enough to absorb.

"I always told him I believed him, but until now I don't know if I ever truly did," Ned said. He munched absently, lost in thought. "It sounds like technology centuries beyond our own."

"I'm not even sure it is technology. That might not be the right word. One theory is that they're sent by the architects of the simulation we live in, checking on their data."

Ned frowned. "I have to call Gilbert."

"Let me speak to him first. I left there last night without waking him. I thought he could probably use the sleep."

Ned nodded, looking at Mason thoughtfully. "Thanks for doing this for him. So many people have told him he's crazy. I think sometimes he just needs to be heard."

"I'm glad I listened," Mason said.

After Ned went back into the office, Mason got his phone and his laptop and sat on the sofa. His call to Gilbert was picked up by a generic "not available" recording, not giving him the option to leave a voice mail. He pulled open his computer, and briefly considered doing more reading about the grays, but he'd already been through a massive amount of material. More interesting right now was the *chaneques*.

Wading through travel and folklore websites led him to more detailed anthropological sources. That word, it turned out, was Aztec, and people in southern Mexico still believed they inhabited the forests. Los Angeles being a Latin American city, it was no surprise to find them here, even though there wasn't a whole lot of forestland. *Chaneques* were said to be quick to take offense at any perceived disrespect. It was lucky for Mason, then, that he'd chosen the right piece of bread, finished his beer when Rudd insisted on it, and agreed to work for Heather. The little people also exacted revenge on those who destroyed flora and fauna. That might explain their concern about a construction project on the other side of town. The general impression he got was that they could be very dangerous when they wanted to be. Don Luís's warning had been well informed.

Next he searched for *brujo* and *coyote,* which led through another labyrinth of material on Latin American folklore. Someone who could take on the form of an animal was called a *nagual.* Coyotes were a popular choice for disguise, but so were birds. The sources said the ability was used to go unnoticed by other people, or to travel quickly. It fit with what he'd seen—a coyote walking around the hills wouldn't merit a second glance, but an elderly man prowling around would have had far more challenges. Don Luís had to be a *nagual.*

It was harder to find any meaningful information about the language skill the *brujo* and the woman at the library had exhibited. There was a lot of fluff about interpreting nonverbal communication through someone's intonation and body language, but that wasn't what Mason had experienced—they had communicated actual meaning to him, parallel with the spoken words. There were other ways to find out about that skill, he decided. Matt spoke Spanish, and Anna spoke at least one other language. They might know.

Folding his laptop closed, he went to the kitchen to make another pot of espresso. He was reluctant to start looking into the construction project that the *chaneques* had told him about. It still seemed hazy, dreamlike, that camp in the woods, but their request was clear in his mind. He had the feeling that once he started, he'd get pulled into it, inexorably, like the moment the doors closed on the train—he'd be on a journey, and there'd be no turning back. He could probably convince himself that the job was untenably vague, and just let it go, if it weren't for his promise, that handshake. He wasn't really afraid of the *chaneques,* despite what he'd read and Don Luís's ominous exhortation. He wasn't on their turf now, so what could they possibly do? But he'd made a deal, and he had to make some effort to live up to it. If he couldn't find the construction site, then he'd think about ditching it.

Pouring the little pot of espresso into his mug, he slurped at it and went back to the sofa. First he looked at satellite images of the neighborhood that Rowan had been talking about. He hoped he was right about which one it was. Looking at a map, it was actually a lot closer to the ocean than he'd thought—the west side of the hill was only a couple of miles from the marina. That had to mean it was the right place, "the hill alone by the sea." The north side of the hill encompassed four different neighborhoods, and there was a lot more open land scattered through it than he'd expected. Some of it was parkland, and some of it was probably too steep or unstable to be developed, but it was impossible to tell from an aerial photo.

The newspaper might be an easier route, he decided, and searched it for stories about impending construction in the area. There was a lot of development going on, but after reading through a long string of articles, only one project fit geographically: a massive condominium complex called The Palms, to be built in Penstock Canyon, an enclave next to Baldwin Hills. He pulled up the address on a map but couldn't find a photo of the property from the street. He could tell that even though the neighborhood was on the hillside, it certainly wasn't a canyon. That had to be a bit of poetic license from a long-ago marketer.

The Palms wasn't under construction yet, but it would be soon, based on the timeline the developer, Douglas Grankin, had outlined for the newspaper reporter. Grankin—that name sounded familiar, he thought. The newspaper article didn't talk about him, and provided no analysis, serving as a puff piece, a breathless announcement of exciting new opportunities to purchase real estate—"650 luxury condos in a clean, safe environment." If it hadn't had a journalist's byline, he would have assumed it was lifted directly from Grankin's press release.

A quick Web search for Grankin turned up a lot of criticism of the man, publicly reviled as a callous mega-developer, and of his projects, derided as "faux-rabian palaces," meaning they were poorly modeled on Arabian design, a widely repeated critique that Mason traced to an architectural preservation group. The photos of his previous work showed sterile mile-long arcades fronting freeway fences, ugly concrete domes and minarets sprouting improbably from densely stacked structures. The windows, each within a false keyhole-shaped Moorish arch, studded the facades claustrophobically close together. Rowan had said something about a sultan's palace—this had to be what he was talking about.

An article in *Va-Voom*, a local alternative weekly, pointed out that in Grankin's architectural renderings of what The Palms would look like, all the sample people in the images, which the writer called "scalies," were white, even though Penstock Canyon and the neighboring Baldwin Hills communities were overwhelmingly African American. The writer speculated that even though it could be dismissed as mere ignorance, perhaps it was an intentional act by Grankin to foment gentrification. That seemed like a stretch to Mason, because wealthy white people displacing wealthy black people didn't really fit the usual problematic aspect of gentrification. Still, it was worrisome, and whether it was intentional or not, that kind of mindset would definitely be greeted with pushback.

Sending the article to Ned's printer, he got up and went to his desk to grab a pad and pen so he could make some notes. Back at the sofa he spent some time trying to find out what stage the project was in, specifically whether it had been permitted yet. It was on unincorporated county land, so the county would be issuing the permits. The county development agency had a confusing, antiquated website that sent him in circles, hunting for promised details that didn't exist, leading him back to the same useless pages again and again. Finally he found the phone number and called them, and after half an hour of transfers, holds, and elevator music, he found the relevant bureaucrat.

"The construction permits are still in process," he said, after a few minutes of Mason listening to him clacking on his keyboard. "But the landscape demolition permit has been issued."

Mason scribbled the phrase on his pad, cradling the phone with his shoulder. "I thought it was an empty lot."

"I said *landscape demolition*," the clerk said, raising his voice and speaking slowly, as if to a simple-minded child. "That means they can remove the trees and brush, that kind of thing."

Rowan had implied that there were no trees, Mason remembered, and there hadn't been any when he'd envisioned the site. It made him question whether he'd found the right piece of land. Everything else had implied that it was. He was going to have to go look at this place, and see whether it matched what he'd seen.

"Do you know when the construction permits will be issued?" Mason asked.

"I can't provide that information."

"Because it's confidential, or because you don't know?"

"I can't provide that information," he said, louder now.

"Is there any kind of environmental review happening, or public consultation?" Mason asked.

"The EIR process begins in two weeks. The public input hearing concerning the EIR is scheduled for next week."

Mason wrote "EIR" on his pad with a question mark. He'd look it up later—no way was he going to give this guy the satisfaction of asking him to explain it.

"Where, exactly, is that hearing, and when?"

"You'll have to contact the meeting scheduling bureau," he said, and rattled off the phone number.

The clerk didn't have any more information about the project, so Mason ended the call and dialed the meeting scheduling bureau. A recording informed him that it was a wrong number, but after a little digging he found the right one on the county website. After another twenty minutes on hold he was able to speak to someone, and when he'd written down the details, he went into the office.

"What's an EIR?" he asked Ned, scanning his notes.

"It means Environmental Impact Report," Ned said, looking up from his desk. "You have to do one before you build anything. Big stuff, like power plants and office towers, not houses."

"Does it have to happen before the construction starts?"

"You can't get construction permits without an EIR, so yeah, the EIR comes first."

"That county twerp could have told me that," Mason said, angry at the realization.

"The county development agency? Why are you talking to them?"

"A client who asked me to look into a real estate development project," he said.

"I don't think you told me about that. What's his endgame?"

"Her. It's kind of a NIMBY thing. She doesn't want a big condo project to get built."

He nodded. "It's next to impossible to stop development for environmental reasons, unless there's an endangered species, and that only happens if you try to dam a river or pave a big patch of desert."

"So it's just a rubber stamp," Mason said.

"Where did you get this client?"

"You know those ads I put on psychic discussion boards?"

"Oh, yeah."

"We met up the other evening. I'm really just doing research."

"Well, don't look to the county bureaucracy for help. You pay their salaries, but they don't work for you—they answer to the developers. You won't get any meaningful information without a lawyer to pry it out of them."

That was a depressing revelation, but Ned ought to know. Mason checked the time, then went to the bedroom and changed into street clothes. He had an appointment with his shrink today, and he was going to have to hustle not to be late. After quickly kissing Ned good-bye, he pulled on his backpack and coasted down the hill to the boulevard, locking up his bike at the metro station. The train came soon enough, which was a relief—he wouldn't be late.

On the way downtown, he thought about The Palms. Heather had asked him to stop the project—she'd actually used that phrasing. But it was so far along already, with the land about to be cleared, that stopping it seemed impossible. Even attempting to slow it down would be a like a gnat trying to stop a freight train. Money was power in this town, and anyone who had built a string of faux-rabian palaces was by definition powerful. Still, he couldn't abandon the mission without pursuing it a little farther. It was the last thing he'd expected when he'd gone to Gilbert's last night, getting hired to investigate a real estate project.

Gilbert, he remembered. He pulled out his phone and called him, only to get the same recorded message. It didn't even ring first. His phone must be switched off.

Climbing up to the street, he admired the building where Miss Cassie's office was, right across the street from the station, a glammy art deco tower that had been restored, its office suites stripped and modernized. Riding up from the lobby to her office always felt like time-traveling, from lavish 1930s mahogany and brass to her twenty-first-century bare concrete and minimalist furniture.

The sign on her door said COME IN, so he slid it over to read PLEASE KNOCK before walking in. Miss Cassie was at her desk, phone to her ear, but she waved him in with a nod. Setting his backpack between his feet, he took his usual spot on the sofa, with a view of the towers of the financial district out the big windows, and waited for her to finish.

Miss Cassie had been his first client when he'd decided to work full-time as a psychic, and in the course of helping her out, she'd somehow railroaded him into becoming her client. But he didn't really mind anymore, as she provided an objective perspective on what was happening in his life, and pointed out things that he couldn't see himself. And he'd never admit it to her, but talking with her helped him keep his ego in check, helped him avoid hubris, and he knew that made him better at his job.

Finally done with her call, Miss Cassie came over and sat in her chair, greeting him with a warm smile and folding open her tablet. She had a bit of weight on her frame but always dressed sharply, today in a navy suit with silver jewelry.

"So how are things going?" she asked, once she was settled.

"Good. I saw someone get abducted by aliens last night."

Her eyebrows shot up as she struggled to mask her disbelief. She began scribbling notes before she spoke.

"I see," she said evenly. "What did they tell you?"

"They didn't see me. If they had, they would have rendered me unconscious, apparently. They're bothering a friend of mine."

"What exactly did you see?"

Mason got into it, describing the waiting in the dark, the appearance of the visitors, the fear he'd felt.

She looked up from her tablet. "What about

your friend? He's aware that this is happening?"

"That's why I was there. He asked for my help with it."

"How are you going to help him?"

"I'm not sure yet," Mason said. "I have a couple of cases that I'm working on right now. I need to ruminate."

"Have you thought about how you're going to process the experience for yourself? It sounds traumatic."

"I think it's fine," he said. "Weird things happen to me all the time."

"That's easy to say," she said, looking up from her notes. "I wonder if you've really sat with the feelings that came up for you."

"I suppose I can take some time to think about it. When it was happening it seemed kind of unreal."

"That's your mind's way of insulating you from trauma," she said, meeting his eye. "It's only a temporary measure, though. Intense emotional experiences will come up again unless you work through them."

"I'm not sure it really was traumatic," he said.

"You said you felt a lot fear and panic. That sounds like trauma to me." She watched him for a moment before continuing. "We have a technical expression in my business: you have to feel it to heal it."

Mason smiled. "I get it," he said, and reached down to pull his notepad out of his backpack. He turned to a fresh page and wrote:

> Feel it to heal it.
> It'll come back to bite you unless you work
>   through it.

A thought struck him. "How's Mrs. Lewis?"

Miss Cassie grinned. "She's fine. Why do you ask?"

Mason had met Betty Lewis when he worked for Miss Cassie at St. Agatha's Episcopal in South LA. The two of them were the church wardens and essentially ran the place.

"I remember that her husband is in real estate development, is that right?"

"He is," she said. "Again, why do you ask?"

"Maybe you could ask him whether he knows this guy named Douglas Grankin. He builds obnoxious residential megaprojects."

"I don't have a relationship with JP directly, but I'll tell Betty you'd like to speak to him. I know she remembers you. I'll have her call."

"Great," Mason said, and nodded appreciatively. Soon their fifty-minute hour was up, and he made his way out, sliding her sign to read COME IN, then rode back down to the street.

■-■-■

Peggy was out rehearsing for her upcoming performance, so he ate with Ned, who went into the office after dinner. Mason was cleaning up when the doorbell rang. He pulled it open to find Gilbert.

"Where were you?" Mason asked. "You weren't answering your phone."

"I had to wipe it," Gilbert said apologetically. "It was spying on me. I got a new number. Do you want to put it in your contact list?"

Mason pulled out his phone and typed as Gilbert recited it.

"You were gone when I woke up," Gilbert said. "When did you leave?"

"Late." He looked Gilbert in the eye. "I saw the grays come for you, man. You were right. You're being abducted."

"You saw them?" he said, incredulous. "I can't believe it."

Ned came out of the office and gave Gilbert a hug. "I'm so sorry about what's happening," he said.

"I'm floored that Mason got confirmation," Gilbert said.

"I'm doing some paperwork, so I'll let you two catch up," Ned said. "We can talk later. Do either of you want a beer or something?"

"Definitely," Gilbert said, and Mason concurred. Ned stepped into the kitchen, returning with two bottles. Gilbert took one and sat on the sofa, and Mason took the other, dropping into an easy chair across from him.

"So what exactly did you see?" Gilbert asked, sipping from his bottle.

Mason explained what had happened, recalling as much detail as he could, and not mentioning Don Luís or the *chaneques*. Gilbert listened intently, interrupting now and again with questions—what had the creatures had looked like, where had they been standing, how had they transported him through the ceiling.

"Do you remember any part of it?" Mason asked.

"Nothing," Gilbert said, and threw up his hands. "But that's not unusual. You have no idea how good it feels to have proof."

"I can hardly believe it myself."

Gilbert sipped his beer. "So what do we do next?" he asked finally.

"There are a lot of abductees out there. I want to do some research and find someone who has had the same kind of experience as you, and maybe talk to them about what to do."

"OK," Gilbert said. He hesitated, and added, "Thanks for believing me."

"I just hope I can help somehow," Mason said.

"Ned and I were going to talk about some business," Gilbert said, rising from the sofa.

Mason nodded and tipped his bottle toward him. "Have fun."

After Gilbert had gone into the office, Mason wondered what business they had to talk about. Ned was trying to get a mortgage, and it was possible that Gilbert would go in on it with him. He really didn't want Gilbert as a landlord, but committing to it himself felt overwhelming.

He eyed his computer, sitting closed on the coffee table. It felt like he'd been working all day, but he did want to find someone for Gilbert to consult with.

Digging around on the Web, he emailed a couple of abduction bloggers, asking for ideas, and heard back from one of them right away, while he was still combing through her posts.

> There are several abduction therapists around the country, and I know some of them are willing to work remotely by video. I haven't worked with him, but I've heard good things about a guy named Kevin Lee in Texas. He calls himself an "experiencer consultant." I know what your friend is going through, and I wish him luck on his journey.

Mason liked her sense of camaraderie, and wrote her a quick thank-you before looking into what the Web knew about Kevin Lee. He didn't have a big footprint online, but he'd spoken at conferences and appeared to be a respected researcher in the field. Mason found his email address and dropped him a note.

> A friend of mine here in Los Angeles is being taken late at night. I witnessed it happening. There were three of them, and they looked like the classic grays. I wonder if you have any advice on what steps he can take to make it stop.

Back on the Web, he read about some of the other abduction therapists, but didn't find anyone else to approach. One therapist in Florida said you could pray the aliens away, which she could be hired to help with, but Mason couldn't believe that organized religion was a solution. A guy in the Northeast made pyramid-shaped sculptures that incorporated specific crystals that he said were proven to dissuade several species of aliens from approaching. The sculptures were pretty, but the claims were too nebulous.

Long after he'd finished his beer, Gilbert and Ned emerged from the office.

"Call me if you find someone I can talk to," Gilbert called to Mason, pulling on his jacket.

"I will," Mason said, rising and joining them at the front door. "I actually just wrote to an abduction consultant. I'll let you know what I hear from him."

"Great," Gilbert said, nodding. "I don't know what I'd do without you two." He pulled Mason into a tight hug, his bristly cheek rubbing against Mason's neck. He did the same with Ned, then said good night.

Climbing into bed with Ned later, Mason couldn't resist asking him about his meeting with Gilbert.

"It's probably none of my business," he said, "but what did you and Gilbert talk about?"

Ned folded his novel closed and turned toward Mason. "He wanted some ideas about buying a house. He has the resources now, with his dad's estate."

"That's great. That house he's in now looks like it might fall in on him."

"The owner doesn't do any maintenance because it was damaged in an earthquake and yellow tagged. I think she's waiting for the property value to go up, and then she'll pull it down and rebuild. For Gilbert, though, it's getting worse. Those stairs are rickety, and the roof leaks."

"Maybe that's because he has a kitchen table and a bunch of potted plants up there," Mason said. "I saw a garden hose too. If he finds a new place, maybe it will have an actual garden for his kitchen table."

Drifting into sleep, he found himself in a dark place, surrounded by little red lights buzzing around him, approaching and then backing off. Maybe they were fireflies, he thought, but they were faster than insects, and bright red. They felt aggressive, and he was afraid that they were going to strike him. He forced himself to wake up, blinking in the dimness of the bedroom to dispel the image. He clicked on the lamp, wincing at the glare, so he could write down the details on his bedside note-pad. "Red lights," he wrote. "Too close. Aliens?"

SIX

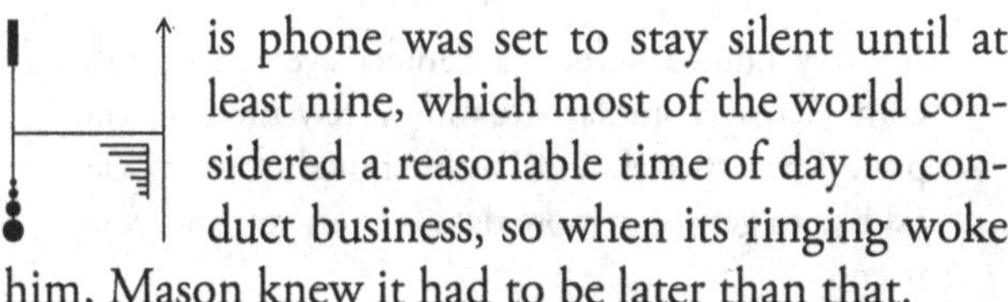

His phone was set to stay silent until at least nine, which most of the world considered a reasonable time of day to conduct business, so when its ringing woke him, Mason knew it had to be later than that.

"Braithwaite," he answered, enunciating as clearly as he could.

"Oh, dear, I've woken you," a woman's voice said.

"Nope. I'm just having breakfast."

"Sorry about that," she said, and it clicked—it was Betty Lewis.

"How are you, Mrs. Lewis?"

"Doing well. Cassie tells me you'd like to chat with JP about a development project. Can you drop by after dinner this evening?"

"That would be great," Mason said.

"Do you remember where we live?"

"I remember the house, but give me the street address anyway." He sat up and grabbed his pen so he could write it down.

"We'll look forward to seeing you," she said, and ended the call.

He sat up on the edge of the bed so that he wouldn't fall asleep again, then pulled on his clothes and went to make coffee, sticking his head into the office to greet Ned on the way past. After ingesting some fruit and starting a second pot of espresso, he went to his desk and opened his computer. Kevin Lee had written back.

> It's very rare to witness a contact event. I've only come across a similar situation a few times in the past. That's special, and I'm interested in your case. I'd like to get some more details from you and your friend.

He took his phone out to the living room, so that his call wouldn't disturb Ned's work, and dialed Gilbert.

"I found a guy for us to talk to," Mason told him when he answered.

"Who is he?"

"I don't know much about him. He's from Texas. He said we can video call him tomorrow."

"Swing by any time, and bring your laptop. I put nail polish over the camera lens on mine."

Mason asked, "Do you have Wi-Fi?"

"Of course. I'm trying to stay under the radar, but I'm not an animal."

Back on his computer he wrote to Kevin Lee to set up a specific time to talk.

He spent the afternoon sprawled on the sofa, looking for other abduction resources, and found a couple of experiencers that might be appropriate contacts for Gilbert. He wrote each of them a brief introductory email. Later on, he looked in on Ned.

"I have a meeting in Leimert Park tonight, so I may have to miss dinner," he told him.

"I could cook early," Ned said, and soon he'd made them each a BLT with coconut bacon. It was delicious, with crispy romaine and sourdough bread.

"So what's your meeting?" Ned asked. "Something about the abductions?"

"It's a friend of Miss Cassie's, about the condo development," he said. "But Gilbert and I are talking to an abduction guy tomorrow morning." He told him about Kevin Lee, and the other people he'd found online.

"I'm glad you're not falling for the New Age stuff," Ned said.

"You don't have to worry. I'm only contacting the ones who use psychology, not Jesus or magic."

■-■-■

Mason rode the metro most of the way to Leimert Park, changing trains downtown and cycling the last few blocks to the Lewises' house. The once-flourishing rosebushes in their front yard had been radically pruned for winter, leaving the house seeming desolate. Mason chained his bike to a street sign and knocked on the front door. Betty Lewis welcomed him in, and had him sit in the front room.

"You have such a lovely home," he said, sitting in a striped wing chair and setting his backpack on the floor beside it. The room was crowded with a lifetime of acquisitions, but not to the point of feeling cluttered, and the dark wood and lush fabrics of the eclectic array of furnishings looked expensive.

"Thank you, dear," she said, smiling appreciatively. "In my day, I didn't have a lot of wealthy African-American peers, so I had to forge my own style."

"I would say it's still your day," he said.

She tittered and touched her necklace. "Would you like some lemonade, or a coffee?"

"Not lemonade," he said quickly. He'd had that the last time he'd been here, and he'd nearly needed dental work afterward.

"Would an espresso do?"

"I'd love that. No sugar."

He scanned the family photos and tchotchkes in the room as she puttered in the kitchen. Soon she returned with a little cup on a saucer, and he thanked her before taking a tentative sip.

"Delicious," he said, trying not to sound surprised. "Better than most coffeehouses."

"I have a good machine," she said, sitting across from him on the ornate settee.

A tall man strode into the room, wearing a suit without a tie. "You must be Mason," he boomed, with the bluster of a businessman.

Mason stood and shook his hand.

"Did Betty offer you a drink?" he asked. He held a tumbler, ice tinkling against glass.

"I'm on coffee, thanks," he said, and sat down again when JP took an armchair.

"So you managed to find your way into the heart of black LA, even at night," JP said.

Mason laughed. "I've been here before."

"Of course, of course," JP said quickly, and sat back. "Plus you have the psychic power. I'm sure that works better than GPS. So you have questions about Douglish? I know him personally."

"Is that how his name is pronounced?" Mason asked. He reached down and pulled his yellow pad out of his backpack.

"Don't write that down," JP said. "It's just what I call him. He has a slight speech impediment, so it's how he says his own name. Plus, he's an ass."

"JP," Betty exclaimed. "Don't you blaspheme in this house."

"Apologies, my dear. I meant to say he's an immoral businessperson. You can write that down."

Mason chuckled, scratching notes on his pad.

"Why are you interested in him?" JP asked.

"I have a client who's concerned about a development in Penstock Canyon. It's called The Palms."

JP nodded. "Yet another faux-rabian palace. Just what South LA needs."

"It looks to me like it's the last bit of green space on that hill."

"Green space doesn't generate revenue, my boy. My concern is that Douglish has no clue about the character of the neighborhood. His monstrosity will bring dramatic change."

"I thought Baldwin Hills and Penstock Canyon were pretty wealthy already," Mason said.

"It's not about income. It's about culture. It's an African-American community, and people are proud of what they've achieved to live there."

"I understand that," Mason said. "My instinct, though, is that any kind of segregation is a bad thing."

"Segregation isn't the issue," Betty said gently. "People have chosen to live in Penstock Canyon, and they've worked hard to afford it."

"Right," JP said. "I just think Douglish should approach the project with more sensitivity to the community."

"*Va-Voom* pointed out that all the people in his illustrations for The Palms were white," Mason said.

"Exactly," JP said. He sipped at his drink and watched Mason.

"Before the Supreme Court struck down discrimination in real estate covenants, this neighborhood was restricted to white people," Betty said, speaking firmly and holding Mason's gaze. "It took decades of personal and legal battles to get to the point that we could even live here."

"Douglish is ignorant of that history," JP said. "He's an ill-mannered steamroller."

Mason sipped his coffee. "My client doesn't want him to build on that land at all."

JP scoffed. "Good luck with that."

It was like Ned had said: development was unstoppable.

"Do you want to meet him?" JP asked.

"Sure," Mason said, surprised.

"I'll make a call. I'm sure Betty has your number, but do you have a business card?"

Mason dug in his pants pocket for a thin stack of them, pulling one from the middle that didn't look too dog-eared, and handed it to JP.

JP examined it briefly, then slid it into his breast pocket. "Give me a day or two," he said.

"I appreciate it," Mason said. He had no idea what he'd say to Douglas Grankin, but he knew he had to take the meeting.

"Well, it was nice to meet you," JP said, rising and excusing himself.

Mason sat down again to finish his espresso.

"What does JP stand for?" he asked Betty.

"We don't talk about that," she said quietly. "It's Roman Catholic."

Mason suppressed a smile. He knew they were Episcopalians, but surely having a Catholic name couldn't be that embarrassing.

"How are things at St. Agatha's?"

"Much the same. We were thrilled you were able to find Sherri."

Mason raised his eyebrows. "I thought that was confidential."

"It is, mostly. The whole thing is very exciting. You actually met with her?"

"I did."

"If you see her again, tell her to drop by. There's always room to heal."

He nodded, then stood and pulled on his backpack. "Thanks for the coffee, and thank JP again for me."

She bade him good night, and he headed out onto the quiet street. An hour later he was home.

"Do you want to watch an episode of *America's Filthiest People*?" Ned asked when he got in. "I saw the preview: the cleanup crew gave the guy the choice between his kids or his houseful of stuff, and he chose his stuff. The kids are in foster care."

"How could I not watch that?" Mason said. "It sounds like television at its finest."

■-■-■

Waking up early, a begrudging concession because he had to go to Gilbert's for the video meeting, he found Peggy sitting at the kitchen counter, eating a bowl of oatmeal, dressed for work.

"Any interesting dreams last night?" she asked him, raising her eyebrows.

"Not that I remember," he said, fumbling with the espresso machine.

"I had a really vivid dream—about you."

He frowned. "What did I do?"

"You were late for work—"

"I don't have that kind of job anymore."

"Mason, it's a *dream*. You're late for work, and you're rushing, and you run onto the stage and get tangled up in all these cables and wires."

"What stage?" he asked.

"At a TV station," she said, talking over the noise of the espresso machine. "You're trying to get untangled from the wires, and you see a spider, and you freak out."

"I'm not afraid of spiders."

"Dude, again, it's not real," she said. "Take a drink of that coffee."

He smiled and brought his mug around to sit with her.

"What happened then?" he asked.

"You're freaking out about the spider, and then somehow a bunch of shredded paper gets dumped on you, and it's blowing all around. Finally you get free of the wires and the confetti and make it to your spot in front of the camera, where you deliver the weather report. You're out of breath and covered in bits of paper, but you manage it. You stand there waving at the weather map, explaining all about high-pressure systems and the Santa Ana winds." She paused and stirred her oatmeal. "Any of that sound familiar?"

Mason laughed. "I have no immediate plans to become a meteorologist."

"It feels important, though. Like it's supposed to mean something."

"I'll think about it today, once I'm awake."

She nodded. "Matt's coming for dinner, and I'm taking tomorrow off to prep for my show."

Peggy left for work, and Mason ate some fruit and had more coffee, eventually feeling lucid enough to head out. He slid his computer into his backpack and kissed Ned good-bye, then cycled to Gilbert's. It looked different in the daylight, less ominous and more dilapidated. He locked his bicycle to the same sign he'd used before and trotted up the stairs, banging on the front door. Gilbert soon answered, waving him in.

"Do you want coffee?" Gilbert asked, pushing his wild hair back and walking into the kitchen.

"Sounds good," Mason said. He sat on the sofa and pulled out his computer. "What's your Wi-Fi?" he called to him.

"It's 'alejate,'" he said, pronouncing it with clipped Spanish vowels, then rattled off the lengthy password.

From where he was sitting Mason could see him preparing the coffee. He pulled two mugs out of the microwave and sprinkled instant coffee into each, then gave them a stir. "You like it strong, don't you?" he asked Mason.

"Yeah."

He dumped more coffee into one of the mugs, not bothering to stir it again, then brought them over to the sofa, handing Mason the one with the spoon still in it.

"I thought you were a Greek coffee aficionado,"

Mason said, sniffing the brown water and giving the spoon a dubious twirl. "Ned always makes it for you."

"He's really good at it, but it's way too much work for me. Don't you need a special pot?"

"Yes," Mason said emphatically. "Ned bought one so he could make Greek coffee for you. No one else ever asks."

"I'm lucky if I can get the microwave working," Gilbert said, waving dismissively.

Mason set his mug on the far side of the table, wiping his fingers on his pants. "Sit over here, and we'll call this guy," he said.

While they were waiting for Kevin to answer, Gilbert sat next to Mason, uncomfortably close, and adjusted the computer so they'd both fit in the video frame. Kevin answered, his corpulent face filling the screen. He wore wire-rimmed glasses and had his hair cut short, military-style. On the wall behind him was a framed poster, dark blue with a series of white dots arranged in a boomerang pattern, and the bold caption PHOENIX 1997.

"Well, howdy," he said, grinning broadly. "Which one of you is Mason?"

After they'd introduced themselves, Kevin said, "It's a pleasure to meet y'all. I understand you've been having a little bit a' trouble with the grays."

It could be authentic folksiness, Mason thought, or it could be exaggerated for their benefit, but either way it made him easy to talk to. Kevin quickly shifted into interview mode, peppering them both with questions, first about Mason's observations on Monday night and then about Gilbert's experiences.

Gilbert had positioned his shoulder in front of Mason's so that he'd be in view of the camera, and gradually relaxed back onto him, putting his weight on Mason's chest. He probably had no erotic intent, Mason reminded himself, but it was still uncomfortable, and he couldn't really shift position without interrupting the conversation.

Gilbert explained that he'd been abducted many times over several years, recently increasing in frequency. He'd discovered an implant in his arm, presumably put there by the abductors, and went to Colorado to have it removed by a specialist.

Kevin sought relevant details: "Do you have any memory of being touched or prodded?" and "Did they communicate anything to you?" He also asked Gilbert things that seemed to Mason way off topic, like "What other strange experiences have you had that didn't involve being abducted?" To Mason's surprise, Gilbert rattled off a couple of incidents that sounded paranormal, even though he couldn't see any connection to the abductions. In one instance Gilbert thought about a specific person and then ran into her minutes later on the street; sometimes he heard Morse code–like beeping, both at home and when he was driving, walking around, or in the market.

Kevin was a skilled interviewer, Mason thought, teasing out information that painted a broader picture of Gilbert's life.

"I think I have a pretty good overview of what's going on," Kevin said finally. "I'm sure I can help y'all with this. My methods involve talk therapy, and maybe some hypnosis."

"I don't think I'm able to be hypnotized," Gilbert said, "but I'm happy to talk."

"I'll email you a cost sheet, and we'll go from there. I look forward to working with you."

"Thanks," Gilbert said. "I'm glad to meet someone who understands this stuff."

"The most important thing to remember," Kevin said, with the air of a teacher, "is that these are your experiences, so you're in charge."

"It doesn't really feel that way when it's happening," Gilbert said.

"I understand that. But there's more than one way to skin a cat."

Gilbert thanked him, and Mason ended the call.

"I love this guy," Gilbert said, finally pulling away from Mason's chest and scooting down the sofa. "I think he really gets it."

"He certainly took the time to get an understanding of your situation," Mason said. "I just wonder if his vision is a bit simple-minded. The abduction phenomenon is nuanced, but he was talking about it like there's only one kind of experience, the nuts-and-bolts physical exam."

Gilbert frowned. "Of course that's what he's talking about, because that's what's happening to me."

"There was the thing about killing cats too. That's how serial killers start out."

"What?" Gilbert looked confused.

"I'm just saying that he seemed like a good fit based on what I saw online, but now I'm not so sure. Maybe we could find someone local. In a city of ten million people, there has to be someone doing this kind of work."

"I can't believe you're being so negative, Mason. He's the guy. Unless his rates are insane, I'm going to hire him."

"That's up to you," Mason said, stuffing his computer into his backpack. "Let me know what you decide."

Home again, sprawled out on the sofa, Mason spent some time looking for a local who might provide the same kind of services as Kevin, but had no luck. He thought about why he wasn't convinced Kevin was the guy. He seemed thoroughly competent, pursuing leads with Gilbert that Mason wouldn't have even thought of, and he was certainly personable, so it had to be something else. It didn't really matter what Mason felt about it, though—it was up to Gilbert now.

Equally pressing was his meeting with Grankin, if JP was actually able to make that happen. In news stories about Grankin's previous faux-rabian palaces he found brief mention of a park he'd created, really just a few yards of grass between the condo and a freeway barrier, but it got Mason reading about the rules around real estate development.

There were surprisingly detailed regulations for residential megaprojects, considering how ubiquitous they were. Among the arcane fire and earthquake safety codes he found an interesting one: planning boards required developers to dedicate a certain percentage of their land to become public parks.

Searching news sources for more details, he eventually found the loophole. There was no requirement as to where the parkland had to be, so developers fully built out land in dense residential areas, then earmarked other property for the parks, in undesirable locations—on steep slopes that couldn't be developed, next to oil refineries and factories, along busy rail lines. Maybe Mason could broach this with Grankin. The guy would probably laugh in his face, but maybe he'd consider turning the Penstock Canyon plot into a park. Asking was no more absurd than the fact that he was doing all this for the *chaneques*. In the light of day, sitting in his own house, the memory of their campfire and tepees felt surreal.

He did some reading about Leimert Park and Baldwin Hills, following up on what Betty Lewis had told him. More than just real estate, schools had been legally segregated well into the 1960s, along with parks, even beaches, and nothing had changed without a protracted fight. The more he read, the more thankful he was to be living now and not then. He was definitely going to ask Grankin whether he'd considered the history of the neighborhood.

Peggy got home in the late afternoon and was soon in the kitchen with her apron on, preparing eggplant lasagna with Caesar salad on the side. Ned worked as her sous-chef. When Matt rang the bell, the savory aroma had already permeated the house. Peggy greeted him with a kiss, and Mason closed his computer and stood up to say hello.

"Do you like ginger?" Ned asked from the kitchen as Matt was pulling his coat off.

"Sure, man, what have you got?"

"Ginger- and lime-infused soda water. I think it's pretty good."

"Fuck, yeah—set me up."

Ned poured glasses for him and for Mason, and the two of them sat in the living room, leaving Peggy and Ned in the kitchen.

"Do you ever feel bad that they do all the work?" Matt asked him.

"Not at all. I help when they ask, and I clean up. Besides, they do it because they enjoy it. There are times when they're not feeling it, and I have to fend for myself."

"You poor thing."

Mason chuckled. "Have you ever heard of someone being able to beam words into your head? Not the actual words, but the meaning."

Matt sipped his ginger water and shifted in his chair. "I would think that if that happened to you, it's about you. You must have been in a receptive state, and picked up the information that was there, rather than the other person beaming it into you."

"It happened twice recently, and both times I was doing hidden mind."

"There you go. It must be a side effect."

"It worked really well, by the way," Mason said, and told him what had happened at Gilbert's.

"No fucking way," Matt said, leaning forward.

"I still hardly believe it myself."

Peggy called to them from the kitchen counter. "Can you two put out forks and plates? The lasagna is ready, and we're finishing up the salad."

The rich, steaming dish was the perfect thing for a winter night, and Mason ate well, enjoying the conversation and the companionship.

"So I'm worried," Peggy said, after she'd finished eating. "I had this crazy dream about Mason, and I think it might be prophetic." She related the story of Mason struggling to get to the stage to do his weather report, screaming at a spider and fending off confetti. The three of them laughed at the imagery.

"I see Mason doing similar things every day just trying to get breakfast," Ned said.

"I'll admit that it's not unlike me," Mason said. "I don't see any particular insights, though."

"Maybe it's symbolic in some way," Peggy said.

"Are you turning psychic too?" Matt asked her.

"No," she said, "but the dream seemed especially vivid. It could be from hanging around with you and Mason all the time. Like the key card for my office: it's just a hunk of plastic until it's in proximity to a power source, and then it's energized. You two are my psychic power source, and

I'm spewing crazy dreams."

"Hopefully the effects aren't permanent," Ned said, a look of mock concern on his face. "I'd hate for their worldview to warp your mind."

"Tread carefully, boyfriend," Mason said. "You're outnumbered."

Ned snorted and turned to Peggy. "So what's up with the performance tomorrow?"

"The dancers are the main thing. Hopefully my music won't get lost behind them."

"It's hard not to focus on the dancers," Matt said. "They're hot."

"Hotter than me?" she asked him, arching her eyebrows.

"Of course not. You're in a completely different category."

"Nice save," Ned said. "You went to a rehearsal?"

"I did," Matt said. "It's really fucking brilliant, at least the part I saw. You'll love it."

They chatted a while longer, and Mason drafted Matt to help clean up, and then he and Peggy disappeared into her room.

Ned came into the kitchen, where Mason was finishing up, wiping down the countertops. "Is Matt staying over?" he asked quietly.

"I saw him take a toothbrush out of his jacket pocket, so yeah, I'd say so," Mason said.

"Has he stayed over before?"

"She's always stayed at his place, I think."

"It's sweet," Ned said. "It means they're getting closer."

Mason nodded. "It's definitely the longest relationship she's had in my memory."

"I just hope having two psychics under one roof doesn't overload the circuits," Ned said, hands on his hips.

"I'll try to dial mine down a little," Mason said.

On his way to bed, Ned called him into the office. "So how long is this antique TV going to sit here?" he asked. "Are you going to use it again?"

Mason had set it beside his desk, the cord piled on top. "I might, yeah."

"Well, it's taking up valuable real estate. Plus it makes me sad every time I look at it."

Mason chuckled. "I'm glad you're so in touch with your emotions. Maybe I can put it in the garage for now."

"Only if it's somewhere it won't fall on my wheels."

Ned's babies were two pristine vintage cars that dominated the garage. Mason was allowed to use a corner, safely away from them, to store his bicycle, and Peggy parked on the street.

"Fine," Mason said, and picked it up. "I was getting sick of looking at it too." He hauled it out to the garage and put it under the work bench.

Climbing into bed, he switched off his bedside lamp, and Ned rolled close to him, folding a leg around Mason's.

"We'll both sleep better," Mason said, "now that all my work-related equipment has been banished from the house. The scouts for *America's Filthiest*

People won't come sniffing around either."

Ned nuzzled Mason's neck. "One day you'll thank me. I'm saving you from yourself."

In the dream world Mason found himself in a TV studio like the one Peggy had related from her dream. There was a map plastered on the wall, and cameras pointed at it. He didn't see any spiders or get tangled in any wires, but he knew it was a dream, and worked to become lucid. He walked around looking at the set. A guy with a pair of headphones around his neck stepped up to him and said, "You're on in five."

Mason envisioned the channel dial on the old TV set, remembering how it felt, the clicking sound it made as it turned. He held out his hand and mimed changing channels. The headphones morphed into a scarf tied on the man's head, shading his neck from the sun, and when he looked around at the studio it was a long covered passageway, open to the sunlight, intense geometric tilework filling the walls. He stepped closer to examine the pattern: brilliant blues and greens and browns.

He was so happy with the success of manipulating the dream that he woke up, clicking on the light and scrawling notes on his pad. "Changed channels," he wrote. "Switched realities."

SEVEN

hy did people insist on calling him so early? He reached for the phone and squinted at the number, struggling to focus his sleepy eyes. There was no name but it was a 213 number, the downtown area code. The phone's clock told him it was later than it felt, almost eleven.

"I'm calling from Mr. Grankin's office," a woman explained after he answered. "JP Lewis requested a meeting for Mason Braithwaite. Can I ask what this is concerning?"

"It's about one of his upcoming projects," Mason said. "The Palms in Penstock Canyon."

"Is this something that can be handled on the phone?"

"It would be better to meet in person," he said quickly.

"Mr. Grankin has a few minutes this afternoon," she said, and gave him the address.

He scrawled it on his bedside notepad, then willed himself out of bed. Peggy was at the front door, guitar case in one hand, garment bag and strap-on fake pregnant belly dangling in the other.

"Can you get the door?" she asked him.

"Where's your boyfriend?" he asked, pulling it open for her.

"At school," she said irritably. "It's almost lunchtime, Mason. Most people are working right now."

"You're not," he said, frowning.

She stopped and sighed, resting her guitar case on the door frame. "I'm sorry if I'm being snippy. I'm just nervous about performing tonight."

"You'll do great," he said. "You always do."

"See you there," she said, and was gone.

After some fruit and a couple of pots of coffee, Mason got dressed and cycled to the metro. On the train he prepared himself mentally for the meeting. The *chaneques'* ask felt completely unattainable, but he had his parkland idea to present to Grankin, and maybe reminding him that it was already a culturally vibrant community would resonate with his sense of civic responsibility.

He surfaced near Miss Cassie's office, amid the glass towers of the new downtown, and walked to the address he'd been given, which turned out to be an ugly aging skyscraper. He'd seen the imposing monstrosity many times but had never been inside.

At the security desk he asked for Grankin's office, and the guard waved him toward the elevators.

"Forty-second floor," she said. "You can't miss it."

When he stepped off the elevator, it was clear that Grankin was the only tenant on the floor, with a massive rendering of GRANKIN & ASSOCIATES filling the wall. He found the receptionist and gave his name.

"Have a seat," he said. "I'll let Mr. Grankin know you're here."

Soon after, the guy led him into the boss's office. Awed by the view, Mason almost overlooked the man himself, standing in front of his desk holding a cell phone to his ear, watching Mason curiously. Two full walls were floor-to-ceiling windows, the city spread out all around. It felt like he was floating above it.

"Nice, huh?" Grankin said, dropping the phone into his suit jacket pocket.

Mason looked toward the desk, finally registering him. He didn't often meet people as tall as he was, and Grankin was thickly built too, an intimidating figure with neatly trimmed gray hair and a deep tan, his face lined by the sun.

"Come closer," Grankin said, stepping over to the windows. He stood with the toes of his shoes touching the glass, hands casually in his pants pockets, and looked over his shoulder, waiting for Mason to join him.

Mason approached the edge slowly, his heart

pounding, knowing his fear was irrational but still struggling to overcome it. Stopping a few feet back, he nodded and said, "Dramatic."

"You have to get right up to it to really appreciate it," Grankin said, watching him intently. "Three more steps."

Mason moved closer, walking heel to toe, like the samurai, not looking down. He felt the tip of his shoe bump against the window pane, his rapid breath fogging a spot on the glass.

"It's perfectly safe," Grankin said softly. "How does it make you feel?"

"Terrified," Mason mumbled.

"You're looking at the sky," Grankin said, still watching him. "Look down."

Mason took a deep breath and cast his eyes downward, seeing the miniature cars snaking along tiny streets far below, feeling his heartbeat accelerating. What was this guy trying to do to him?

Finally Grankin stepped back, breaking the spell. Relieved, Mason turned away from the window. There were no chairs, he realized, just the one behind Grankin's big desk.

"So you're a friend of JP Lewis," Grankin said cordially, leaning back on the front of his desk and folding his arms. "You know he's a crook, right?"

"He's a personal connection," Mason said. "I don't really know about his business dealings. I did some work for his wife."

"I bet she's got him whipped, huh?"

"It doesn't seem like that to me." He could feel the

blood still coloring his face. "Why don't you have any chairs in here?" Mason asked, glancing around.

"So that people can't waste my time," he said. "Which brings us to the twelve-dollar question: what do you want?"

Mason chuckled. "Just twelve dollars?"

"Based on the estimated value of your shoes."

Mason glanced at his feet. Granted, his sneakers were old, but what kind of way was that to judge someone?

"What do you think these babies are worth?" Grankin asked, holding out one leg and waggling his foot. His shoes were flashy, absurdly elongated, and made out of some kind of animal skin dyed yellowy-tan.

"They look like what mid-level Middle Eastern royalty would wear to chase women at clubs on the Sunset Strip. Seventy thousand dollars."

Grankin guffawed. "Not quite that much," he said. "Now, who the hell are you?"

Mason fished in his pocket for a business card and handed it to him.

"A psychic?" Grankin said, scanning the card and frowning.

"I've been hired by people who are concerned about The Palms project in Penstock Canyon," he said.

Grankin's face hardened. "You're one of those NIMBY fucktards," he snapped.

Mason tried not to react, meeting his eye. "Not really," Mason said. "I was hoping—"

"Trust JP-fucking-Lewis to throw something like this at me. Godless bastard."

"Godless? I think he's an Episcopalian."

"Exactly," Grankin said. His nostrils flared. "Listen, you little fuck. You think you can come in here and insult me? I know how to handle you people." The speech impediment was noticeable for the first time, and Mason felt droplets of spittle land on his arm.

There wasn't going to be a conversation about the virtues of public parks and cultural wealth, Mason realized, but he willed himself to stay civil. "That sounds ominous," he said, and folded his arms.

"Believe me, you mooky orangutan—if you fuck with me, I'll ruin you."

"I'm not here to fuck with you," Mason said.

Grankin reached back and picked up his desk phone. "Security," he growled into it, and slammed it down again.

"There's no need for that," Mason said, trying to keep his voice even. "I just wanted to talk about one of your projects."

Two uniformed guards stormed into the room and stood menacingly close to Mason, but they didn't touch him, so he didn't move.

"You don't know anything about my projects," Grankin said, glaring at him. "I built this town from the ground up, with my bare hands."

"That sounds a little hyperbolic," Mason said.

"Hyper what?" he demanded, but didn't wait for an answer. "Throw him out."

The guards each grabbed an arm, pinning them roughly behind his back.

"There's no need for this," Mason told them, stumbling as they pushed him toward the door. "I'll go willingly."

They ignored his words and dragged him into the elevator, not loosening their grip. The receptionist watched them go but didn't look especially concerned. Mason tried to wrench his arm away from one of them, but the goon just pulled harder, inflicting such pain in his shoulder that Mason let his arms go slack. They were smaller than he was, but it didn't matter—they knew what they were doing. It was alarming to be controlled so effectively, to be completely powerless.

"You can let me go," he said, trying to sound calm. "I'm not going to resist."

Neither one of them spoke, maintaining a firm grip. When the elevator doors opened they hauled him into the lobby, then frog-marched him out to the street, where they finally released him, shoving hard so that he tumbled to the sidewalk. One of them had somehow pulled off his backpack, and threw it in Mason's face.

"Was that really necessary?" Mason shouted. "Do you kiss your mother with that mouth?" It made no sense, as neither one of them had uttered a word, but he was so addled that it was all he could think of. They weren't listening anyway, disappearing back into the building.

Sitting up, he found his hands were scraped, and

his pants were torn at one knee, where there was a little blood. Pedestrians were maneuvering around him, some staring furtively, some ignoring him. A guy in a delivery uniform stood at the curb, his dolly laden with boxes, watching him with interest as he got to his feet.

"Remind me never to piss off anyone in there," the guy said.

Mason ignored him and hobbled toward the metro station, processing what had happened. By the time he reached the platform, the stiffness was gone from his knees, and his shock had become anger. He seethed half the way home, imagining his revenge. He closed his eyes, willing himself to calm down. JP had warned him that Grankin was immoral, but he hadn't expected that to extend to him.

The house was empty when he got in. He peeled off his clothes and jumped in the shower to wash off the grime of the sidewalk and the toxic residue of the whole encounter. Emptying the pockets of his shredded pants, he dropped them in the kitchen trash, then went to the sofa and pulled open his computer. It didn't take long to uncover more dirt on Grankin.

None of the stories involved indisputable evidence of wrongdoing, the kind of thing a prosecutor could use, but it was easy to read between the lines. Grankin had once had a disagreement with a development partner about a building that was almost finished, and after a few weeks of stalemate, the structure had mysteriously burned down. Grankin recouped his losses in insurance payouts, but his partner was left with a burned-out empty lot.

Years earlier, he'd built one of the faux-rabian palaces forty feet taller than the zoning allowed, and the city wouldn't sign off on a final inspection, leaving the completed building empty for months. A city council member finally pushed approval through a committee, allowing the building to open. The councilman's children soon had anonymous scholarships to an exclusive private school, and his home was renovated and expanded by a helpful contractor, unsurprisingly linked to Grankin.

Someone who could buy politicians and torch buildings as part of doing business clearly wielded a lot of power. Mason was probably lucky that all he'd lost was a pair of pants.

When Ned got home he was dressed for meetings but carrying several bags of produce.

"I thought the farmers market was yesterday," Mason said, rising and kissing him hello.

"I stopped at a different one," he said, piling the bags on the counter. "I was on the Westside. How does steamed fennel sound for dinner?"

"Amazing," Mason said, and perched on a stool.

"If we eat now, we won't be rushed to get to Peggy's thing." He put his apron on over his dress shirt and set to work.

Mason was going to tell him about meeting Grankin, but before he could get into it, Ned opened the trash bin.

"Are these your pants?" he asked, his brow furrowing.

"Sadly, yes. I loved those. They're from the thrift store, so they're irreplaceable." He related the encounter with Grankin—standing with their noses to the window, the sudden flash of aggression, getting the bum's rush to the sidewalk.

"Were you hurt?" Ned asked, concern in his eyes.

"Just my pants."

"What an asshole."

"I went through the whole conversation in my head, and I can't think of anything I said that could have set him off. I'm thinking maybe there's more to it that's not about me, like something between him and JP Lewis that I don't know about. Maybe throwing me out was a message to him."

"Maybe," Ned said, pulling out the fennel bulb and setting it in a colander. "But Grankin definitely has a bad rep in my field. I've heard mild-mannered real estate people call him a sociopath. I hope you're not planning to go back there."

"Not a chance," Mason said. He decided not to repeat Grankin's most disquieting comment, "I'll ruin you." As threats went, it wasn't very specific. Still, he'd given the guy his business card, which meant he knew how to find him.

After they'd eaten, Ned asked, "The Crown Vic, or the Barracuda?"

"We're going to be parking behind an abandoned hospital in Lynwood in the dark. The

Crown Vic probably projects less of a 'steal me' vibe."

"Wise choice," Ned said, and soon he'd pulled the roomy old sedan out of the garage. He navigated to the freeway and eased into the stop-and-go evening traffic.

"The more I think about that guy and his thugs, the angrier I get. And what was the thing about making you stand at the window?"

"I think he got off on seeing my fear."

"What a freak." Ned deftly changed lanes, glancing in his side mirror. "Bullies—they think they can do whatever they want."

"I'm trying not to be angry about it. It doesn't seem constructive."

Ned glanced at him, surprised. "Good for you."

"I do wish I had some idea how to shut down his project in Penstock Canyon, though. I was going to pitch the idea of turning it into parkland, but I didn't even get the chance."

"The only way to derail it is grassroots opposition," he said. "NIMBY groups have to get big media attention and lots of public support before any politician will side with them over a developer. Otherwise, the one with the money always wins. But if there's a threat to getting reelected, that can sometimes trump money."

"I haven't seen any coverage of opposition to this project, so that route seems unlikely."

"Keep digging," Ned said. "You've achieved unlikely things before."

They pulled up at the abandoned hospital, and a man clad in black, his woolly cap embroidered with SECURITY, waved his flashlight, pointing out an opening in the weed-choked chain-link fence that led into the driveway. Ned eased the car through the narrow gap and parked in the dark lot.

"It looks so sketchy," Mason said as they got out. "At least there are some other cars here."

"It'll be fine," Ned said, locking the Crown Vic. "It's Lamar's event, and he's a security guard. I'm sure his colleagues will keep an eye on everybody's wheels."

"There's Peggy's car," Mason said, spotting her Prius. "And Matt's."

"Which one is Matt's?"

"Guess," Mason said.

Ned looked around. "The SUV with the roof rack," he said.

"Very good. You could be a detective."

"You want the full profile?" he said, looping his arm through Mason's as they walked toward the dark hospital. "It's six years old, which means he's not showy. I also detect laziness. Most people would have pushed out that little dent on the fender. And he needs to take that thing to the car wash."

"Damn," Mason said. "Not bad."

A dim light in a doorway guided them into the building, and they followed a couple of other spectators through the long empty foyer, its paint peeling, linoleum shredded and torn. They climbed a flight of stairs and found several rows of folding chairs set out in a semicircle.

"This was an operating room," Ned said. "Look at the equipment."

Hanging forlornly from the ceiling on an adjustable arm was an array of lamp hoods, the bulbs long removed. Other than that, only a couple of metal sinks on a tiled wall were left from the room's former life.

Quite a few people were already seated, and Matt caught their attention, waving to them from the side of the room and pointing to seats he'd saved for them.

A hush fell over the crowd as the room fell into darkness, and then a spotlight winked on. A man stood in the beam, dressed as a doctor in a white coat, complete with a stethoscope. He stood perfectly still at first, then slowly began to move, undulating rhythmically. As the lighting came up he was joined by a woman, also dressed as a doctor, and then three more dancers, dressed in scrubs. The medical garb didn't hide the fact that they were agile and very fit. Matt was right—they were hot, and effortlessly fluid.

Their movements were elegant, and Mason could tell they were well-rehearsed. The five of them were mesmerizing, performing energetically without any music. Two of the dancers went into the next room and came back wheeling an old-fashioned hospital bed that bore their roommate, propped up on the mattress, wearing a medical gown over her massive faux baby bump and Peggy

Pregnant's signature headband, a ring of little daisies.

Mason glanced at Matt, who was watching her intently, a broad grin on his face.

She winced in discomfort, massaging her belly. Her escorts parked the bed facing the audience, and another dancer nimbly presented Peggy with her guitar. She strummed tentatively for a few seconds, then launched into a song, as the dancers temporarily retreated.

The sound was powerful after the silent visual intensity of the dance, Peggy's upbeat folk music filling the room, her voice booming despite her recumbent position.

> You're all the drugs I need, darlin'
> To put me on a high
> Medicated by your love
> I call you my feel-good guy

After her vocal part the dancers came back, and she played guitar through the last act, a comfortable backdrop for the more leisurely, flowing choreography, and the focus shifted again to the moving bodies. Finally it was over, and the audience was on its feet, clapping and cheering wildly.

Mason and Ned congratulated Lamar, the choreographer, who was beaming with the success, and said good-bye to Matt, who wanted to see Peggy afterward. They talked about the event on the trip home, parsing the meaning of it, and which of the dancers had better chops, and Peggy's performance.

Mason was exhausted from the events of the day, and once he made it to bed, he quickly descended into sleep.

Ned looked shocked when Mason wandered into the kitchen the next morning. He was sitting at the counter eating berries out of a bowl, and glanced at his watch.

"Do you know what time it is?" he said. "I just got up myself. Do you need medical assistance?"

"Time and tide wait for no one," Mason said, shooting him a look and spooning coffee into the espresso machine.

"That only applies if you're planning to catch a boat."

"I'm actually going to look at Grankin's site in Penstock Canyon."

"What will that accomplish?"

"Probably not much. But after tangling with his goons yesterday, I'm motivated to do something."

Ned nodded. "I see that."

Mason grinned sleepily and ate his breakfast. A few doses of espresso later, he pulled on his back-pack and cycled down the hill, surprised at how cold it was so early in the day. He boarded the train with his bicycle and traveled west, then cycled the last mile or so up the hill to the Penstock Canyon neighborhood. The streets were quiet, and the houses were sprawling bungalows, set back with lots of greenery.

He had no trouble finding the lot where The Palms was slated to be built. He stopped to look at it, breathing hard from the climb. It looked exactly as it had in his mind's eye with Rowan, the crest of the hill looming in the distance higher up, and as Rowan had said, it was an open field, no trees or structures on it, not even a chain-link fence to separate it from the street.

A black-and-white poster stapled to a utility pole caught his eye. "No palaces in Penstock Canyon," it read. "Wake up, people. Stop out-of-control development." It was the first opposition he'd caught wind of, and it made him smile. It was encouraging to see it plastered here. There was an email address at the bottom, so he pulled out his phone and wrote a quick message.

> I saw your poster in front of The Palms site. I'd like
> to find out what's being done regarding the project.

It didn't look big enough for a 650-unit building, even though it was larger than a typical city lot. He walked onto the land. He could see why the *chaneques* were attached to it—the property had a pleasant slope, out of view of the neighboring houses, and it bordered directly on the scrubby parkland above. Were they here now, he wondered, invisibly exercising their property rights?

He wondered if a psychic reading was in order. It didn't seem likely that he'd be able to pick up any insight from the land itself, but he decided it was worth a try. He knelt on the earth and closed his eyes, working to clear his mind, making it receptive to whatever inspiration might be floating around.

A memory popped up, of standing on the precipice in Grankin's office, looking at the streets far below. He pulled back involuntarily, mentally thrown off balance, and opened his eyes. That wasn't an image he wanted to dwell on.

Taking a last look at the open field, he got his bike and headed down the hill. A woman was walking up the street toward him, her mass of hair bouncing with each step. She hailed him as he approached.

"Are you Mason?"

"You must be from the antidevelopment group," he said, stopping and sliding off his seat.

"That's right," she said, looking him over suspiciously. "Who are you working for?"

He thought quickly. He couldn't very well tell her that he was working for concerned neighbors, because she'd ask who they were, and he certainly couldn't say anything about the *chaneques*. "No one. I'm just a concerned about the issue."

She folded her arms. "Concerned as in looking to buy into The Palms?"

"Why do you instantly think 'gentrification' when you see a white guy?" he demanded. "I don't have any money."

She frowned and cocked her head. "I didn't realize you were white. I would have said more of an orangey-pink. Is 'sunburned' a color?"

Mason laughed. "It is in my world," he said, and

met her gaze. "I'm not here to buy anything. I was hoping to help stop The Palms from getting built."

"Why do you care?" she asked.

"Well, I have some connections to the neighborhood. I did some work for Betty Lewis and Cassie Millar at St. Agatha's in Leimert Park."

She nodded. "I don't go to St. Agatha's, but I know Betty's people. JP is a pillar of the community."

"I was at their house on Wednesday," Mason said. "They're concerned about displacement too. What is your group doing to stop Grankin's palace?"

She watched him for a few seconds before replying. "Do you drink coffee?"

"I'm a hardened addict."

She smiled. "My kitchen door is right over there."

She turned and started down the hill, and Mason wheeled his bicycle between them.

"I'm Janice," she said.

"Nice to meet you. You already know my name."

"We started No Palaces when we first got wind of the project," she explained, leading him through a wooden gate into an overgrown yard, where Mason leaned his bicycle against a bougainvillea hedge, then followed her into her kitchen.

"Sit," she said, and pulled two mugs out of the cupboard, then filled them with steaming brew from her coffeemaker. "How do you take your coffee?"

"Black," he said.

Janice grinned and slid one of the mugs toward him, sitting down across the kitchen table with the other. Mason could tell from the aroma that it was quality stuff.

"What do you know about the project?" she asked him.

"I know it's steamrolling its way through the county planning bureaucracy right now. I know that Douglas Grankin is a trash bag."

She nodded. "He's the king of dirty tricks. A conservancy group was trying to get historic status for an old building downtown a couple of years ago, and he demolished it overnight, before the decision was made and before he had any permits to do anything. His response to the city was 'Whoops,' but of course the deed was done, and he went ahead and built one of his palaces there."

"Couldn't they fine him?"

"Whatever fine they got from him would have been recouped a thousand times over when the building opened to tenants." She sighed. "I know we're not going to be able to stop this one, but at least we can speak up at the EIR hearing. Do you know what the EIR is?"

"I do," he said. "My understanding is that an unfavorable environmental report could shut down a project like this."

"It's possible," she said. "But the report is prepared by professionals, usually academics. And guess where their funding comes from?"

"Industry," Mason said glumly, sipping his coffee.

"Right. The public hearing is just a political concession to NIMBYism. Neighbor objections aren't going to have any impact on the report."

"That's so depressing. You're the only person I've met who's against this, and you're telling me nothing can be done."

"I don't want to make it sound completely hopeless," she said, wrapping her hands around her mug. "We're definitely going to the hearing to speak up against it."

"How many people are in your group?"

"It's mostly just me," she admitted. "I see a lot of these cases in my day job, and now it's happening on my block."

"What's your day job?" he asked.

"I'm a lawyer. I do environmental work, so I know what questions to ask." She stood and ducked into the next room, returning a moment later with a business card.

Mason glanced at it briefly, and saw that she worked downtown. He didn't recognize the name of the law firm.

"That's my number," Janice said. "Call me if you want to come to the hearing. It's on Thursday."

"Thanks," he said, and fished his own card out of his pants pocket and handed it to her.

She read it and laughed. "I wish you could use your psychic power to thwart this whole mess."

"So do I," Mason said. He rose and thanked her for the coffee, then retrieved his bike and cycled back to the metro, enjoying the easy downhill ride.

It was nice to have found someone else who wanted to stop the project, but clearly she felt as powerless as he did. To achieve the broad-based grassroots opposition and media coverage Ned had described would require a team of full-time activists, not a lone lawyer with a full-time job elsewhere. Getting that kind of attention was going to take more than him and Janice and her staple gun.

EIGHT

I t was late afternoon by the time he got home and had some leftovers for lunch. Ned was out doing Saturday errands, and Peggy was likely making the most of her day off. Mason was enjoying the quiet house, considering taking a nap, when Gilbert called.

"Do you want to come with me to the airport?" he asked. "I'm picking up Kevin."

"He's coming here?"

"Yeah, man, he's in the air right now."

"Wow—I thought he'd work with you by video."

"He says he needs to be here with me. It would be nice to have you there when I meet him, if you're up for it. I can pick you up."

"Sure," Mason said. It would give him a chance

to get a better perspective on the guy, to see if there was a reason for his wariness about Kevin or to put it to rest.

He sent Ned a text telling him what he was up to, and got a text from Gilbert a few minutes later that he was out front.

When Mason went outside, Gilbert's car was nowhere to be seen, but a full-size SUV with tinted windows was blocking the garage doors. The driver's window slid down, and there was Gilbert, grinning broadly.

"Where's your car?" Mason asked him, climbing up into the passenger's seat.

"Sold it. This is my new ride."

"This?" He glanced back into the cavernous cabin. "That was such a sensible car."

Gilbert pulled out of the driveway and headed down the hill. Mason felt like he was riding in a bus.

"You want me to buy one of those plug-in sewing-machine cars, like Peggy? I live on a hill. It needs to be able to make it up there."

"This thing looks like a tank," Mason said.

"I know, right? She's a beauty."

Mason hadn't meant it as a compliment. "Did you add the window tint? It doesn't look legal."

"That's from the factory, so it better be."

Soon they were on the freeway, and Gilbert merged into the carpool lane.

"So did Kevin explain why he had to come out here?" Mason asked.

"He says he needs to see my circumstances, and pick up on the vibes. Also I think therapeutic stuff works better face-to-face."

"It sounds like you've already hired him."

"I bought his ticket and paid him for two days' work. We'll go from there."

"Was the trip his idea?"

"What difference does that make?" Gilbert said, glancing over at him.

"I just wonder if he's taking advantage of you. You know, so he can come out to California, hang out at the beach."

"Dude, he's not going to the beach—it's freezing. And it's not a scam. He's going to help me."

"I hope so."

Gilbert scoffed. "It's sweet that you're being protective, but I'm not a dummy. I think I'll know if I'm getting conned."

That was easy to say, Mason thought, but he knew that Gilbert tended to believe almost any crazy story that came his way.

Soon they were crawling along in the throng of vehicles at LAX.

"There he is," Gilbert said, and swung the massive car over to the curb.

Kevin stood waiting with a wheelie bag, wearing ill-fitting jeans and a dark jacket. He was tall, and with his weight, quite imposing. He smiled and held up his arm in greeting when Mason rolled down the window.

At least he just had a carry-on, Mason thought.

But then Kevin reached around and wrangled another suitcase, twice the size of the wheelie. Clearly he was prepared to stay beyond the contracted two days.

Gilbert shifted into park and opened his door. Mason jumped out too, to help with the bags.

Kevin smiled and lifted his carry-on into the back of the SUV. "I would have recognized y'all anywhere, Garfield, with that orange mop of yours," he said, his drawl even more pronounced than before.

Mason heaved the big suitcase in and frowned at him. "You can just call me Mason."

"Sit up front with me," Gilbert said to Kevin, and to Mason, "Is there room for you in the backseat? I haven't actually sat back there yet."

"There's room for a whole dance troupe, plus the choreographer," Mason said, climbing into the middle seat.

Gilbert wove his way out of the tangle of roadways around the airport and got on the freeway. They chatted amicably about Kevin's trip, and the culture shock of landing in such a crowded place.

Even though Gilbert was in the carpool lane, traffic slowed to a crawl.

"There must be an accident," Kevin said.

"It's just afternoon traffic," Gilbert said.

"Already?"

Gilbert nodded. "Oh, yeah. It's basically from three to eight Monday to Saturday."

"How on earth do you live here?" Kevin asked,

turning to Mason and raising his eyebrows.

"We roll with it," Mason said.

"Not very fast."

"Mason actually rolls on two wheels," Gilbert said. "He cycles everywhere, so the traffic doesn't affect him."

Kevin guffawed, and then looked from Gilbert to Mason. "Y'all aren't kidding. You have a car too, though, right?"

"I don't," Mason said, and smiled thinly.

"Now I've heard everything. A Los Angelean without a car."

"We're called Angelenos," Gilbert said, glancing over at Kevin.

"That sounds kind of Hispanic."

"Not really," Gilbert said, grinning quizzically at him before turning his attention back to the stop-and-go traffic. In the rearview mirror, Mason thought he saw the stirrings of doubt in his eyes.

"Well, when in Rome," Kevin said. "Staying with you will be an opportunity to see how you people do things." He chuckled. "You Angelenos."

"You're staying at Gilbert's?" Mason asked, leaning forward. He hadn't expected that. His place was so grungy, and there was no spare bed.

"Yep," he said, looking back at Mason. "That's where the action is, so that's where the work is done."

"So what exactly are your skills?" Mason asked, trying to sound nonchalant.

"I call myself an experiencer consultant, and also

a life coach. I help people who are having contact experiences figure out what's happening to them. It's an intensely personal journey, but I provide gentle guidance so that they can calm down, get better rest, and integrate the contact into their regular lives."

"Great, right?" Gilbert said, looking at Mason in the rearview. "That's exactly what I need."

But Kevin hadn't explained what techniques he used.

Gilbert parked in his driveway facing uphill. The suitcases tumbled out when Mason opened the back of the car.

"Careful with those," Kevin said, chuckling and taking his wheelie bag.

Gilbert trotted up to open his front door, keys in hand, leaving Mason to haul the big suitcase up the stairs.

"Thanks, partner," Kevin said as Mason heaved the bag across the threshold. "Where's the bunkhouse?"

Gilbert gestured toward the back of the apartment and walked into the bedroom, Kevin following with his luggage.

"This ought to work just fine," Kevin said when he returned, looking around the apartment.

Gilbert went to the kitchen and returned with three bottles of beer, handing one to each of them and then sitting in his easy chair. Mason waited for Kevin to sit on the sofa before joining him at the other end, worried that the worn old thing might collapse with both of them on it.

"Cheers," Kevin said, and reached over to clink the neck of his beer bottle against each of theirs.

"So what's the plan?" Mason asked, eyeing him.

"I'm going to stay close to Gilbert and help him maintain awareness during his encounters," Kevin said.

"How are you going to avoid getting switched off, or taken too?"

"I'm able to stay awake when they appear," he said. "I've never tried to stay out of sight, like you did, but I can watch. I'll also work with Gilbert to prepare for the visits, and then work through it with him after." He took a long drink from his bottle. "For me, getting involved is part of the process."

"Isn't there value in trying to stay objective?" Mason asked.

"If you're there, you're involved," he said, meeting Mason's eye. "There's no way to be objective."

Mason nodded. It reminded him of what Miss Cassie had said, that he had to feel his way through such intense experiences. It made more sense than keeping them compartmentalized.

"So when the visitors come," Mason said, "what exactly do you do?"

"That depends on how the abduction plays out." He smiled confidently. "I do what needs to be done."

"Right," Mason said, and looked away. It sounded suspiciously vague.

"I'm glad you have a decent-size bed," Kevin said. "At least we'll be comfortable."

"You're going to sleep with him?" Mason asked, incredulous.

"I have to," he said. "My rule is, be there, be aware."

Mason shot Gilbert a questioning look.

"There's nothing hinky about it, man," Gilbert said. "I'm straight."

Mason's eyes narrowed. He'd never been convinced that was completely true.

"Me too," Kevin said quickly. "It's for work. There's nothing gay about it."

"Not that there's anything wrong with gay," Mason said, holding his gaze.

"Of course not." He smiled amicably. "Since we're all here, I wanted to ask you some more about the night you saw the grays. What did it look like when they took Gilbert through the roof?"

Mason explained what he remembered, and Kevin asked a series of questions, gently probing for more. It felt like he was asking him to repeat himself, the same thing stated in a slightly different way, describing the elongated blur of the spindly creatures and Gilbert's frozen form moving upward and disappearing. But by talking about it, the memory was getting sharper. He had to admit Kevin had a canny ability to pull out detail.

"What about the mental technique you used?" Kevin asked, switching topics. "How is it that they didn't sense you?"

Mason explained how he had induced hidden mind and answered Kevin's questions about it.

"I wonder if you really were hidden," Kevin said finally, "or if they knew you were there, and knew you thought you were invisible, and so they left you alone."

"What would be the point of that?" Gilbert asked.

"I suspect they have something planned for Mason."

"That's disconcerting," Mason said. "I hope they're not as clever as you think."

"Who knows," Kevin said, shrugging. "But keep me apprised of your experiences."

Kevin started in on Gilbert, asking him the same kind of probing questions. Mason excused himself and summoned a ride-share on his phone, declining Gilbert's offer to drive him home.

"You guys have work to do," he said, and let himself out, waiting for the car in the dark at the bottom of Gilbert's driveway.

The last thing he needed was to start worrying about aliens coming after him. He closed his eyes and took a few deep breaths, clearing his mind. He wouldn't have thought of that possibility himself: that they had known he was there, and had been playing him. It almost sounded paranoid. Hidden mind had been effective—Don Luís hadn't seen him either, and he'd been able to see the *chaneques* when people usually couldn't. That whole evening had been a riot of paranormal activity.

His ride arrived, a sensible little black car, dwarfed in the driveway by Gilbert's obnoxious hulking SUV. He got in beside the driver and fished for the seatbelt.

"Out drinking tonight?" he asked cheerfully.

"No," Mason said. "I've been helping a friend who's been abducted by aliens."

He expected a sidelong glance and a quiet ride home, but the driver just nodded. "It's more common than people think," he said, expounding on the issue as he navigated the residential streets toward the boulevard. He didn't have any ideas that Mason hadn't already read about, but he was well versed in the field. Mason mostly listened, fascinated that the topic was so ordinary for this guy.

"My aunt is an abductee," he said as they pulled onto Mason's street. "She's cool with it now, though."

"How did she get to be cool with it?" Mason asked.

"She says the aliens have a purpose for her. Something about helping others. She does volunteer work now."

"I hope my friend can be that successful," he said, digging in his pocket for his wad of cash as they pulled up to his house. He tipped the guy a few dollars and went inside, relieved to be home.

Ned was lounging on the sofa, reading a book, and set it face-down on his chest when Mason came in.

"How did it go?" he asked.

"Dude seems to know what he's doing, and

Gilbert's happy that he's here." He dropped onto the sofa at Ned's feet. "He's going to sleep in Gilbert's bed with him. To be close to the action, he said."

"That's a little odd," Ned said, "but Gilbert's not shy about things like that."

"Doesn't it seem suspicious that he's paying the guy, and the guy is freeloading at his place, drinking his beer, sleeping in his bed? Am I the only one who sees red flags here?"

"I wonder if Gilbert will have trouble maintaining boundaries," Ned said. He put his book on the coffee table, and Mason wrapped an arm around his shoulder.

"Of course he will," Mason said. "The guy will be right there in his bed."

"Is this Kevin guy hot?"

"Not to me. Maybe to Gilbert," he said, running his fingers through Ned's thick hair.

"Gilbert's straight," he said.

"Everyone keeps saying that."

Ned chuckled. "Not everyone thinks like you do. You think beds are only for sex. That's so conventional. There are other uses."

"Like monitoring alien abductions."

"Exactly. Speaking of sex, I've been thinking about it a lot this evening. Are you up for it?"

"Of course—as long as we stop talking about Gilbert and his bedmate."

"Do you know if Peggy is out for the evening?" Ned asked.

"I'm not sure."

"In that case, maybe we should take it into the bedroom." He stood up and stretched.

Mason rose too, catching Ned's eye. "That's so conventional."

* * *

Waking late in the morning, Mason found himself alone in the house. He made coffee and was sitting at the counter eating some grapes and an apple when he got a text from Ned.

> Sunday lunch with the family. Gilbert and Kevin are coming for dinner.

That'll be interesting, he thought, and sent back a quick acknowledgment.

One of the psychic techniques he'd learned on a recent case was astral projection. Matt had explained it as shifting awareness to another location, rather than some part of his essence leaving his body, but either way Mason had found it difficult to stabilize the experience and not succumb to the fear of getting permanently separated. Alone in the quiet house was a perfect opportunity to try it, so he stretched out on the sofa and got comfortable.

Traditional Chinese practitioners of the craft had useful advice: get rooted in your body before you go. He focused on the feeling of the sofa cushions, the position of his arms and legs, knowing he could recall the feeling and return safely if necessary. Next he focused on projecting his essence—"a tight white ball of qi," one of the sources had described it—up through the top of his head.

It took a while, and he drifted close to sleep, but eventually he felt himself floating upward toward the ceiling, able to see the room from above. He could see himself lying on the sofa, eyes closed, neck at a weird angle, but with the shock of that image he instantly crashed back into his body. He had to move away more quickly, he realized, pushing aside the feeling of fear. He shifted position and cleared his mind again, then repeated the process, forming a memory of his physical position, willing himself upward. *Baldwin Hills,* he told himself. *Let's go there.*

Drifting into a dreamlike state, he found himself floating up again. He thought about Penstock Canyon, the street where he'd met Janice—and then he was there. From above he could see the land where The Palms was to be built, unique in its emptiness, and the winding streets and houses of the neighborhood. It wasn't scary, like Grankin's office windows, maybe because his actual body wasn't at risk, or maybe because of his altered state of mind. *There's Janice's house,* he thought, *and her garden. That bougainvillea is out of control. She probably doesn't have time to take care of it herself, working downtown all week. She should hire a gardener.*

That wasn't why he was here, he remembered, and pulled his focus away. *Higher,* he thought, and he zoomed upward, the street and the houses shrinking. He struggled not to panic, knowing that would snap him back to his body. Instead he focused intently on the scene below. Other times in this state he'd been able to see ley lines, invisible bands of energy that ran all around the earth, and he looked for them now, willing his mental focus to look below the surface. Before, the lines had looked like glowing white threads, but nothing like that was visible here. Instead he saw a black bubble under the grassy plot, extending beyond it, under the houses, under several streets, under the parkland higher up the hill.

A big black bubble, he thought dreamily, suspended there in the earth, instead of ley lines. How far did it go? He thought about getting a wider view, and instantly he snapped upward, the city receding below. It was terrifying, the sudden change in perspective, but he tried to suppress his concern, focusing on the landscape. The black expanse permeated the city, darker in some spots, lighter in others. Is it everywhere? he wondered, and with that he accelerated farther upward, but before he could take control of the experience, he crashed into his body, opening his eyes and inhaling sharply.

He sat up and looked around the room, making sure he was really here, waiting for reality to stabilize. He hadn't seen the ley lines, even though he knew they were there—and what did the blackness mean? He closed his eyes and remembered the scene. Lush gardens and lawns, Janice's wild bougainvillea, the *chaneques'* land, scrubby open parkland nearby, and on the far side of the hill, roughly gouged earth and mule-head pumps—an oil field. Rowan had mentioned that, the endlessly nodding machines.

Oil. Was that what he'd seen? The entire LA Basin was essentially floating on a pool of oil, and there were pumps and pipelines everywhere. Crude oil even seeped out of the ground in places, into basement parking garages, sidewalk cracks, lawns. Maybe it meant something.

Getting his laptop from the office and returning to the sofa, he researched local oil deposits. They'd been exploited for centuries, it turned out, and there was still plentiful crude, even under neighborhoods where the derricks had long ago been dismantled, replaced with city streets and buildings.

There wasn't a comprehensive listing of the local oil deposits, and forgotten capped wells even turned up from time to time when landscapers started moving dirt. Extensive information about the location and volume of oil pockets was only available for sites that had featured in legal battles, when all the research had been revealed in the court proceedings and had become public record. The lawsuits were usually between homeowners concerned about noise and pollution, and oil companies anxious to exploit a dwindling resource.

He couldn't find anything about oil under Penstock Canyon, although the field on the other side of the hill was well documented. A two-year-old news article about one of the lawsuits said that oil companies had all kinds of information about what was under the ground, but kept it secret from their competitors, out of the public eye unless it was subpoenaed. The state land bureau kept some historical records of seismic surveys and core samples, the journalist explained, but those files were all on paper, and the bureau was under no obligation to share any of it with the public.

When Ned came in, he closed his computer, grateful for the interruption.

"How does white bean chili sound?" Ned asked, taking off his jacket. "And butter lettuce with lemon dressing."

"I love that chili," Mason said. "I'm sure everyone else will too."

Soon Ned was at work in the kitchen, declining Mason's offer to help. The main dish wasn't especially laborious, and he was almost finished when Gilbert and Kevin arrived. Mason opened the door, and Ned came out to meet Kevin. They were still standing there, chatting, when Peggy got home.

"Whoa—scrum at the front door," she said as she walked in.

"Good to see you," Gilbert said, stepping over and kissing her on each cheek.

"Hi there," she said, spotting Kevin.

Gilbert introduced them, and Mason shepherded them to the sofa, then joined Ned in the kitchen.

"Do you drink red?" Mason asked, holding up a bottle that Ned had handed him.

"Looks good," Gilbert said.

"Wine?" Kevin asked. "That's too fancy for me."

"It's actually not," Mason said. "This brand is famous because it only costs two dollars a bottle."

"Maybe you have beer?" Kevin asked.

"I have Singha or Belgian," Peggy said, rising from her chair.

"I thought we were still in America," Kevin said, smiling sweetly. "I'll take anything that tastes like American beer."

"Belgian," Peggy said confidently, and went into the kitchen.

Mason opened the wine and poured glasses for Gilbert and Peggy, then sat on the other wing of the sofa with his own. Ned brought out a bowl of hummus and a plate of crudités, setting them on the coffee table.

"Ooh la la," Kevin said, examining the food.

Ned chuckled and sat cross-legged next to the coffee table, taking a couple of carrot sticks from the plate. Kevin sipped appreciatively at the beer Peggy set in front of him, then took a slice of red pepper and swiped it through the hummus, sniffing it audibly before taking a bite.

"Not bad," he said. "Have some rabbit food, partner. The dip is pretty good."

"Don't you love that?" Gilbert said. "He calls me 'partner.'"

"It's very sweet," Peggy said. "It sounds like you two are bonding."

"Probably," Gilbert said. "I think I just needed support with all this crazy stuff that's going on."

Kevin picked up his beer and said, "Cheers."

They all raised their glasses, except Ned, who raised his empty hand, curled around an imaginary glass.

"You're not drinking?" Kevin asked him.

"I'm in recovery," Ned explained.

"Oh, I'm so sorry," Kevin said, his eyes growing wide.

"I'm not," Ned said. "My life is great sober. Better than it's ever been."

"Cheers to that," Mason said, and lifted his glass again, catching Ned's eye.

"So you're an abduction coach," Peggy said, sipping from her wineglass.

"Yes, ma'am," Kevin said, and explained his work, using the same vague language he had with Mason.

"How was the first night of observation?" Ned asked.

"I didn't get taken, but we talked a lot," Gilbert said. He looked at Kevin, admiration in his eyes. "Kevin has a lot of experience. He's helped a lot of people."

"I'm looking forward to hearing what happens during an abduction," Mason said.

"It won't be long," Gilbert said. "I can kind of feel it looming."

"Dinner's basically ready," Ned said, and stood up, urging them to sit around the table. He went into the kitchen and loaded bowls with chili and plates with salad onto the bar. Mason helped him distribute everything before they sat down.

"It's delicious, Nedly," Peggy said, savoring a bite.

"I agree," Gilbert said. "It's so nice to have decent vegan food."

Peggy looked at him in surprise. "That's new."

"I've gone mostly vegan," he said. "Ned finally got through to me."

"You'll feel better," Ned said. "But you should be doing it for yourself, not for me."

"Good for you, man," Mason said between mouthfuls. "What do you mean by 'mostly'?"

"I'm completely vegan now, except in my sleep."

"You're eating steak in your dreams?" Peggy asked.

"It's when I'm on Ambien. I wake up and find empty candy wrappers, snack treat bags, and cheese dust on my fingers. Once I found a microwave burrito wrapper from the convenience store."

"You sleepwalk to the store?" Mason asked.

"I guess."

"I can't believe you take Ambien," Peggy said. "You're so anticorporate."

Gilbert's face clouded. "I need it to get to sleep when I feel the aliens coming around."

"We're working on that," Kevin said. "The plan is to get him completely off it."

"That sounds like a good idea, if you're sleep-shopping," Ned said.

"This is good chow," Kevin said to Ned. "I'm surprised how tasty it is without any meat."

"There's more, if you'd like," Ned said.

"I can't eat that much," he said. "When I heard you were cooking without meat, I stopped and had a couple of corn dogs."

"This guy," Gilbert said, grinning. "They were tacos."

"But this is good," Kevin continued. "Almost as good as real food."

"Thanks so much," Ned said, leaning back in his chair. "That means a lot coming from a corn-dog connoisseur."

"We hadn't eaten since the buffet at church," Gilbert said hastily.

"You went to church?" Ned said, surprised.

"At my insistence," Kevin said. "It's a good habit to get into."

Ned bristled visibly, but before he could speak, Peggy cut in.

"Let's not go there," she said. "Remember the rule about dinner conversation?"

"I wonder who you voted for in the last election, Kevin?" Ned said, his tone even but his eyes burning.

"We tend to elect very different people than you do in kooky California, that's for sure," he said, raising his eyebrows.

"What did I just say?" Peggy demanded. "Both of you: no politics, no religion."

Kevin looked chastened, and Ned looked away.

"Tell us about your hometown, Kevin," Mason said. "I've never been to Texas."

Kevin nodded and picked up his beer. "Well, as

you know, East Texas has the finest climate this side of paradise," he began.

Mason sat back, relieved that Peggy had managed to defuse the looming squabble. He found himself being drawn into Kevin's lilting dialect. He was a skilled orator, Mason thought, like a classical story-teller, his choice of words eloquent, his style engaging. The place sounded magical, and he wanted to go there now, getting lost in Kevin's imagery of beech forests and rolling green countryside.

When he'd finished, Mason helped clear the table, and Ned brought out some fruit, his ire seemingly having evaporated.

Later on, when their guests were leaving, Ned and Mason walked out with them.

"Where's your new wheels?" Ned asked. "You could have parked in front of the garage."

"Up the block," Gilbert said.

"Gilbert let me drive his rig," Kevin said, "and a car was blocking your garage when we pulled up. Some guy was sitting in it, writing on a clipboard."

"I wonder who that was," Ned said. "What kind of car was it?"

"A blue one."

"You're really not from around here, are you," Ned said.

Kevin cackled and slapped him on the back. Ned winced at the blow but smiled and waved good-bye as they walked down the street.

"Who would be clipboarding in our driveway?" Mason asked as they went back into the house.

"Are we being surveilled?"

"I wouldn't worry about it. I'm sure it's nothing sinister," Ned said, wrapping an arm around his waist. "You're starting to sound like Gilbert."

"I'm realizing that Gilbert's usually right."

Peggy was in the kitchen putting things away, and Ned went in to help her.

"You're always the sensible one," Mason said to her, climbing onto a stool at the counter.

She grinned at him. "Wasn't it nicer not to get into a brawl?"

"Much nicer," Ned said. "Thanks for that."

"I'm just glad you and Tex were both able to keep a lid on it," she said.

Ned nodded and put his hands on his hips. "You know, I think I've experienced maximum Kevin."

"He certainly wasn't afraid of expressing his opinions on how we eat," Mason said.

"Food is emotional for everyone," Peggy said.

"He thinks we're snobs," Ned said. "Wine and foreign beer, fresh vegetables. It's exotic to him."

"I'm not a snob," Peggy said. "I don't get paid enough to be."

"Is it a red-state thing?" Mason asked.

Ned shook his head. "That's a stereotype. People in Texas drink wine and eat lettuce. The stupidity is all him."

"I don't think he's stupid," Peggy said, frowning. "He expresses himself well, and he already seems to be working out a road map for Gilbert."

"Ignorant, then," Ned conceded. "Anyone who

gets sucked into a religion has fallen for a con."

"I'm sure religious people don't see it that way," she said.

"Whether you like his beliefs or not, he seems to be helping Gilbert," Mason said. "He was an emotional wreck when I met him downtown last week, and now he's chatty and cracking jokes. That has to count for something."

That night, drifting into the hypnagogic state, Mason dreamed he was in Gilbert's bed, unable to move, surrounded by the three bug-eyed visitors. He tried to scream but couldn't, and felt his body floating up toward the ceiling. He woke up, heart pounding, looking around the dark room to make sure it had been a dream. He clicked on his bedside light and scrabbled for his pen, writing down the details. Kevin's dark thought came to mind, that the visitors might have plans for Mason. That would be a real nightmare.

"Not cool," he said aloud, looking at the chair in the corner, and the closet door, clearing his head for a few minutes so that he wouldn't fall back into it.

As he drifted into consciousness he could hear Ned arguing with someone. Only one side of the conversation was audible. He had to be on the phone. Mason couldn't parse the words, muffled by the closed office door, but he listened for a few minutes anyway, trying to work up to facing the cold world outside the covers. Ned definitely sounded upset. He never argued with people in his work. His job wasn't like that, and he wasn't like that.

Bracing himself, Mason got out of bed and pulled on his clothes, then went out to the kitchen to make coffee. He overheard Ned as he walked by the office door.

"How is that possible?" he demanded. "The numbers are the same as they were a week ago."

Mason was partway through his first pot when Ned's conversation ended, so he went to the office and opened the door.

"That sounded intense," he said.

"Did I wake you?" Ned asked abruptly, still wound up from the confrontation.

"I'm not worried about that. I never hear you yelling at people."

"It was my mortgage broker." He did a neck roll, and spoke more gently. "She's acting crazy. I've known her for years, and we've been talking about this deal for months, and suddenly she changes her mind about my eligibility. It makes no sense."

"Is it going to mess up the transaction?"

Ned considered that. "I hope not. I'll have to find someone else to do it, though, which is a pain."

"Did she tell you what changed?"

"Nothing changed," he said emphatically. "There's no reason. I know all about this stuff, and how it works. There's no new information. It's something about her."

"Do you want to come out and have a coffee, maybe cool off?"

"Thanks, sweets, but I really have to focus on this," he said, rubbing his eyes.

Mason murmured assent and closed the door. It was worrisome—Ned rarely got that stressed out.

He took his computer to the sofa and did some more research about the local oil industry. The fact that he'd seen the oil fields in his astral projection had to be significant, but he wasn't sure what it meant. He read about the dozens of players pumping crude oil out of the ground, some owned by the conglomerates and others small local businesses. Regulation was spotty, with some rules applied at the municipal level and others enforced statewide. Like most oversight, the rules were primarily responses crafted after accidents, disasters, and civil lawsuits.

The mailbox rattled, and Mason closed his computer and went to the door to get the mail, sorting through it on his way to the office. Ned always got way more, but today there was an official-looking letter for Mason too. He handed Ned his stack and sat at his desk, sorting through the junk and advertising, and then tore open his lone letter.

"Fucking royal fuck," Ned snapped.

Mason looked up at him in surprise. "Bad news?"

"It's a vermin control inspection notice from the county." He read from the sheet in his hands:

> Based on a resident complaint, we are dispatching an
> inspector to your address, next Monday or Tuesday

> between 7 am and 4 pm. The owner or leaseholder
> is required to be present to grant full access.

"What kind of vermin?" Mason asked.

"None that I know of." He scanned the sheet and flipped it over. "They don't specify."

"Could it be that skunk that was hanging around last spring?"

"That's considered wildlife, not vermin. It has to be about bugs or rodents."

"What resident would complain? That seems strange too."

"I've no idea. I guess I'll have to be home those days."

"If you have meetings, I could probably handle it," Mason said.

Ned sighed. "It's interesting that they can't do anything about the sixty thousand people sleeping under overpasses, but they have the resources to come into my house because some gossipy neighbor saw a roach."

"I got my own coffee-spilling letter," Mason said. "It says 'Notice of tax default.' Can you decrypt this?"

Ned reached for the page and read through it. "It's a shakedown," he said finally. "They say you're running a business in the city without a business license." He handed the letter back. "Did you get a business license?"

"No, but I don't make that much money."

"You still need a license."

"What will they do?" he asked, looking at the letter again, with its imperious black title.

"They're not going to sue you," Ned said, his tone softening. "It's just a piece of paper. Go downtown when you have some time and sort it out. Business taxes are miniscule compared to payroll taxes. You'll owe them, like, thirty dollars."

"It's weird that all this stuff is happening all at once," Mason said. "Your broker, and the vermin, and the tax thing."

"It's just a coincidence, nothing woo-woo." He attempted a grin, but he looked tired.

Mason nodded. There was no reason to add to Ned's stress level. He slid his tax notice into a desk drawer, then went to the kitchen and made another pot of coffee, taking it out through the French doors to stand on the balcony. It was too cold to work out here, and the neglected chairs were accumulating winter dust and grime, but it was nice for a few minutes with a warm mug in hand. Ned stuck his head out to say good-bye, on his way to a meeting downtown.

"Curry for dinner?" he asked.

"Sounds great," Mason said, and watched him leave.

Ned might reject the possibility that the coincidence was meaningful, but Mason knew there was often more going on. What looked coincidental often wasn't; events were linked by the unseen forces running through the world. What connections could there be among their volley of bad news?

They'd come from completely different sources.

Grankin. The idea struck him with sudden force, and he felt a surge of adrenaline at the thought. Of course. He was entrenched in the real estate industry, and dealt with local governments as a matter of course, trading favors to get his monstrosities built. Grankin had threatened him, but why would a busy man bother following through with someone as insignificant to him as Mason? He thought about it, sipping his espresso as he looked out over the hilly neighborhood. Grankin had proven himself to be a petty egomaniac, not just with Mason but in well-documented dealings with other people. He wondered how many visitors to his office had been thrown out on the street. In the pit of his stomach he knew that his hunch was right.

If Grankin had orchestrated these annoyances, it was harassment, and it made him angry. Instinctively, he wanted to fight back. The problem was that he had no way of doing that. The only remotely satisfying action within his reach was to interfere with The Palms, and the only lead he had on that was the nebulous vision of the oil field.

Back on the sofa he looked up the state land bureau, digging through their website for records about Penstock Canyon, but there was nothing specific, no publicly accessible databases. One of the articles he'd read said older land records were still kept in paper files, so he found a phone number and called the land bureau's main office in Sacramento.

"I'm interested in looking at seismic and core sample records for a neighborhood in Los Angeles," he explained.

"Who do you work for?" the bureaucrat asked.

"No one," he said. "I live down here, and I'd like to find out what's known about the mineral resources."

"I see," she said, and the long runaround began. He was transferred repeatedly to a series of lines, sometimes getting a busy signal or a voice mailbox. Asking for a number each time before he was redirected, he called back several times, but never got anywhere. He finally decided to give up when he called back and it rang once, then quickly disconnected, the bureaucrat on the other line apparently not willing to talk to him anymore.

It was frustrating, but maybe there was another way. He looked through the names of the slew of small local oil companies he'd seen earlier, and picked one that sounded inconspicuous. Dialing the land bureau's main number again, he cleared his throat as he waited for the receptionist to pick up. It might have been one of the people he'd talked to earlier, but she didn't seem to recognize his voice.

"I'm legal counsel to Brigid Petroleum in Los Angeles," he explained, "and I was trying to track down some documents in your collection."

"You should talk to someone in the mineral assessment department," she said. "They're responsible for records and archives."

That was new—the first time he'd been sidelined

with the public information office, which had been reticent to provide any information. Moments later he was talking to a man who identified himself as the department head.

"We have our own in-house data, of course," Mason said, after he'd repeated his fake identity, "but I'm trying to track down state records on a plot of land in LA County."

"Is this the first time you've done this?" he asked.

"I'm embarrassed to admit it, but yes, it is," Mason said, his heart pounding. "I'm new to this job."

"Not to worry. You'll get the hang of it," the guy said amicably. "Land data went digital in 1996. Anything older than that is on paper. All our archival records for Southern California are kept at our office in Fort Ronnie."

"Do you have a number for that office?" he asked, and jotted it down.

"What kind of exploration are you doing?" the bureaucrat asked. "Looking to drill, or just speculative?"

"Listen, I've got another call coming in," Mason said. "But I'll be in touch."

He hung up and sat back on the sofa, amazed at how quickly things had changed. He'd gotten farther in five minutes posing as a corporate flunky than he had in an hour as himself. The ultimate goal of accessing the records might be more difficult if it was going to require the same degree of subterfuge, but he hadn't even expected to get this far.

It made more sense to pursue the paper files rather than trying to get access to the newer database, he decided, which would surely involve more stringent controls and verification of his employment. Paper archives were like libraries, not subject to hacking, and therefore their guardians were much less concerned about granting entry.

The phone number he'd written down started with 213, the downtown area code. A Web search didn't turn up a specific listing, but other numbers with the same prefix all belonged to the state government.

"Fort Ronnie" turned out to be the nickname state employees had given their massive downtown office block that bore the name of Governor Reagan. Mason knew the building well: it was a blight on the city, a dark and sterile dead spot in an otherwise vibrant part of the city. The nickname fit—it was indeed fortress-like, with no access at sidewalk level, just blank walls and shuttered windows. It was textbook fascist architecture, designed to dominate the neighborhood and alienate passersby.

He dialed the number, and a woman answered.

"Violet Hernández."

"My name is Braithwaite," Mason said, using his real name in case he had to show them his ID later, "and I'm legal counsel to Brigid Petroleum. I'd like to make an appointment to come in and take a look at some of your files."

"I'm the chief archivist," Violet said. "Are you talking about seismic data?"

"Seismic and core samples," he said, hoping that was the right answer.

"What quadrant, and what date range?"

"Uh, I don't have the quadrant information in front of me," he said, thinking quickly. "The site is in LA County, near Baldwin Hills."

"More important is the date," she said. "Were you looking for database access?"

"We're interested in older stuff," Mason said. "Pre-1996."

"You'll definitely have to come in, then. What company did you say you worked for again?" He heard paper rustling in the background.

"I've been through all this with the head of your department in Sacramento," he said. "Do I really need to repeat every detail to you?"

"Of course not," she said deferentially. "And you don't need an appointment. Come in any time after ten. We're on the ninth floor."

"Thanks," Mason said, and smiled to himself as he hung up. It had been risky to feign impatience, but it had worked. He had no idea if the oil records would yield anything of value, but at least he was a step closer to finding out.

⬛-⬛-⬛

Peggy got home after work and chatted with him for a few minutes before disappearing into her room. Not long after, Mason heard a knock at the door. At first he wasn't even sure it was a knock, but it came again, louder this time. That was a little strange, as most people just used the bell. Darkness had fallen, as it did early on winter days, so perhaps their visitor had overlooked the button.

He got up off the sofa and pulled open the door to find a man wearing a black suit and a fedora. Even though it was dark out, he wore mirrored aviator sunglasses.

"What's up?" Mason asked, standing in the entrance. He didn't want to be too cordial, in case the guy was selling something, or worse, a missionary—they often dressed formally.

"You need to keep your nose out of things that don't concern you," the man said, his voice even and emotionless.

"What?"

"Stay away," he said, in the same tone.

"I'll do whatever the hell I want," Mason said, angry now. "Tell your boss he doesn't run this town."

"You know too much."

"I know I'm going to call the cops if you don't get off my porch," Mason said, raising his voice.

The man stood there, not speaking for several seconds.

"Did you hear me?" Mason demanded. It wasn't difficult to stand his ground, as the guy was half a head shorter than Mason, and he hadn't even raised his voice.

"Most people are more fearful than you are," he said, unmoving, his tone still flat and dry.

"I won't be intimidated by you," Mason said,

folding his arms. He could feel the blood throbbing in his temples.

"Stay away," the guy said evenly, and then turned and walked away.

"You said that already," Mason shouted after him.

He pulled open the door of a car, parked in front of the garage, big and black, with heavily tinted windows, darker even than Gilbert's. Mason watched it pull away. It was old, he saw, but he didn't know what make it was. Ned would know. He memorized the details so he could ask him about it.

"What's all the shouting?" Peggy asked, coming into the living room.

"That developer I went to see is harassing me," Mason said, closing the door. Peggy sat with him on the sofa, and he told her about the visitor, and Ned's broker, and all the bad news in the mail. He spoke rapidly, still amped up from his encounter.

"If the developer is behind it all," she said, "why is he going after you with all these passive things, and then sending a wimpy thug to your door as direct intimidation?"

"Does it have to be logical?" Mason asked. "He's a sociopath."

"Just think about it for a minute," she said. "What exactly did the guy at the door say to you?"

Mason went through it with her, repeating the conversation.

"Why would he say 'You know too much'? I thought you didn't have any dirt on Grankin's new palace. That's why you can't do anything to stop it."

"It was an odd thing to say," he admitted.

"And he's wearing a dark suit and driving a vintage black car. Does that sound like Grankin's people?"

"He's probably a subcontractor."

"Mason, think! It's not about Grankin. It's about Gilbert." She held his gaze and lowered her voice. "You know too much about the abductions."

He thought about that, and realized she was right. His hands suddenly felt cold and clammy.

"Say something," Peggy said.

"You think he was from some three-letter agency?" he said slowly.

"How would I know? You're the psychic. Did he seem like a bureaucrat to you?"

"Not any more than he seemed like a real estate guy." He watched her for a moment, lost in thought, willing himself to be rational. "It explains why he said most people were more frightened of him. I didn't realize it was about that, so I wasn't fearful at all. And there *was* something eerie about him—the sunglasses, the way he talked. But I see strange people all the time."

"Because you ride public transit," she said.

"It's true—the other day there was a guy on the metro with no pants, just sitting there in his skivvies. 'I'm on my way somewhere, why would I need pants?'"

Peggy snorted.

"I've seen a lot of weird stuff lately. The aliens

weren't the only thing I saw that night at Gilbert's." He told her about Don Luís disguised as a coyote, and the *chaneques,* and visiting their camp.

"My god, man," she said finally. "Ned wondered who your client was, but he didn't want to be too nosy. I can see why you didn't tell him." She watched him for a minute, concern in her eyes. "What happened that night?"

"A cluster of weirdness erupting into the ordinary world. Like when you poke a fire, and a whole bunch of sparks fly up all at once."

"It's still happening—the guy in the fedora is just the next weird thing."

"Thanks for helping me see that," Mason said. "I was so hopped up about the developer that I missed it, but you're right, he's definitely connected to Gilbert's abductions. It comes up a lot in the literature, the man in the hat intimidating flying saucer witnesses."

"Does the literature say who he is?"

"There's no consensus. Some authors say they're shadowy government agents, and others say they're aliens. This guy didn't seem like either, just … different."

"You don't seem that freaked out," she said. "I would be. He threatened you."

"His message was 'Stay away.' I'm doing that anyway. Kevin is working with Gilbert now. My part in it is finished."

She nodded. "Are you going to tell Ned?"

"Not right away," he hedged. "He's got a lot on

his plate. I haven't even told him my suspicions about Grankin yet."

Ned got home soon after, and Mason was glad to see that he seemed less stressed out than earlier in the day. As promised he made a lentil curry for dinner, with cauliflower on the side. When the three of them sat down to eat, Mason broached his theory.

"Is it possible that your mortgage person changed her story this morning because someone pressured her?"

"That might explain it," Ned said. "But who would do that? I don't have any enemies."

Mason sighed. "I do. When I was in Douglas Grankin's office, he said 'I'll ruin you.' It's the kind of thing a bully would say in anger, so I brushed it off, but now I'm thinking maybe all the bad stuff that happened today was from him."

"It's shocking to think he would go so far," Peggy said, a cauliflower floret poised on her fork.

"What I don't get is how he knew about Ned," Mason said. "Siccing the city tax people on me would be easy—I gave him my business card. But how did he find you?"

"A quick background check would turn up your home address," Ned said, "and then me, and that I had a real estate transaction underway. He could have found out who my broker was with one phone call."

"I wonder if he'll go after me," Peggy said. "I live here too."

"Oh, god," Mason said. He hadn't even considered that.

"I doubt he would, because you work at a law office," Ned said. "Lawyers have tools to defend themselves. It's like when a coyote is looking for dinner—he'll go after the rabbit rather than the skunk, because the skunk has defenses. Mason and I are the rabbits, and you're the skunk."

"Thank you," Peggy said. "So reassuring, and so eloquently stated."

Mason looked at each of them. "I'm so sorry you got dragged into this."

Ned shrugged. "If Grankin did this, his point was to demonstrate the reach of his power, and to scare you off. He'll be confident that he's accomplished that because you haven't gone after him again. He'll let it go."

Mason nodded. "You're being so calm about it."

"It's all fixable," Ned said, gesturing widely. "He doesn't control every broker in town. The county won't find any vermin, so that's just a one-time waste of my workday. The business license is on you. You'll have to fix it, but it's a minor detail."

"You're such a good man," Mason said, leaning back in his chair. "I feel calmer just hearing you talk about it."

Ned smiled. "I'm glad. Don't let one bully get you all freaked out."

"I'm not afraid of him," Mason said. "But I'd love to shove back."

"You said it yourself—that's not constructive," Ned said.

"Well, The Palms, then, I'd love to shut that

down. I've done some research about the oil that's under the land. It might be a way to influence the EIR."

"Good idea," Ned said.

Is your client concerned about Grankin specifically?" Peggy asked.

"They just want the land to remain undeveloped."

"Great," she said. "You can forget about him, and approach it however you want."

■-■-■

After dinner Peggy practiced guitar in her room, which always filled the house with rich, warm sound that mellowed Mason out. He helped Ned clean up, carrying dishes from the table to the counter.

"I saw this old car today," he said. "I wonder if you can identify it."

"Did you get a picture?"

"No, but I remember what it looked like."

"Maybe you could draw it," Ned said.

Mason went to the office to get a notepad and a pen, and sat at the counter with him. He sketched the grill and the hubcaps.

"That looks like a New Yorker," he said. "Were the headlights covered?"

"They flipped open when he started the car," Mason said. "There were four of them."

"Did it have wheel pants?"

"What are those?"

"A cover over the top half of the back tires."

"I think so, yeah."

"Definitely a Chrysler," Ned said. "Mid-seventies."

Later the music stopped, and Peggy wandered out. "How do you feel about vegan macarons?"

"I'd eat them," Mason said, looking up hopefully.

"I know *that*," she said, and laughed. "I was wondering if Ned wanted to try to make them."

"I'm game," Ned said, and soon the two of them were in the kitchen, discussing the chemistry involved. It had something to do with garbanzo liquid, but Mason didn't hang around to watch, retiring to the office.

Sitting at his desk, he filled a page of his notepad with what he remembered about the visitor with the sunglasses: his outfit, his car, what he'd said. Reading through it again, he felt the hair on his neck stand up. Maybe this was what Kevin meant when he said the visitors had more in store for Mason. He shuddered and pulled out the folder about Gilbert's visitations, slipping the notes into it. He read through the file, then added some notes about Kevin—his impressions, what little the guy had said about his work with Gilbert.

Then he made some notes about the oil business and his interaction with the state land bureau, clarifying things in his head. He stuffed the pages into the folder he'd labeled PENSTOCK CANYON, then slid both folders into his drawer.

He decided he should check in on Gilbert, and pulled out his phone. It would be too late to call most people, but that kind of rule didn't apply with him.

"How are things going?" Mason asked when he picked up.

"I think we're making a lot of progress," he said. "Kevin has hypnotized me twice now, and we're pulling out a lot of information. He's taping the sessions so I can hear them after. It hasn't all coalesced yet, but I think we'll get there."

"He hypnotized you?" Mason asked. "I tried that. It didn't work."

"Well, he has more history with experiencers. Maybe he has some specialized technique for people like me."

"I guess that's reasonable," Mason admitted. "Just think carefully about everything he's telling you, and be sure that it makes sense."

Gilbert laughed. "None of this stuff makes sense. You know that."

NINE

Waking early to his alarm, Mason forced himself out of bed and ate a bowl of oatmeal and fruit. He put on the only decent office drag he had, a 1950s-style suit and tie. He'd recently acquired it working a case for some scientists. It felt like wool, but they had made it out of a futuristic fabric that always managed to retain its shape.

Assessing himself in the floor mirror in the bedroom, he found the transformation dramatic. He wouldn't be out of place even in the most uptight office. The sheen on the gray material looked smart, even though the necktie was a bit wide, and its olive-green hibiscus print felt dated. There was a hat that went with it, but he decided against wearing it—he'd look like the weird guy who had knocked on the door last night. In the office he picked up his backpack, but realized he couldn't really wear it if he wanted to pose as a well-heeled lawyer. There was always Ned's briefcase, but no— he couldn't imagine lugging that around all day. He'd have to live without his notepad, and make do with what fit in his pockets.

"You look so sharp," Ned said, turning from his desk. "You should always wear that."

Mason laughed. "You like it because it's wrinkle-proof. It's the only thing I own that doesn't instantly come untucked or look disheveled."

"You always look fine," Ned said. "But that suit is superfine."

After Mason said good-bye, he tied a Velcro strap around his pant cuff to keep it out of his chain, then pulled out his bicycle and cycled to the metro. He locked up his wheels before catching the train, as it was a short stroll from the station downtown to Fort Ronnie.

Walking in the financial district, he felt a little nervous, thinking about his subterfuge. He never wore a suit unless he was up to something like this—just wearing it felt dishonest. When he looked down, he saw the bicycle strap still around his pant leg, and pulled it off and stuffed it in his pocket. He wasn't really out of place here, he reminded himself. Looking at the other office workers, he knew he blended in, which gave him confidence.

When he found the entrance to the fortress he

got in line to go through the metal detector with the horde of bureaucrats arriving for work, putting his keys and his phone in the little tray and stepping through, smiling idly at the guard, then riding the elevator up to the ninth floor. It didn't take long to find the door marked LAND BUREAU ARCHIVES, but before he walked in, he took a few deep breaths to calm himself down. He had no qualms about posing as someone he wasn't, but he had to be composed enough to pull it off.

In the little front office was a receptionist behind a desk, and behind that a closed door. She looked up and greeted him with a smile, her eyes flicking down to his necktie.

"I'm here to see Violet Hernández," he said, and recited his name.

"I'll let her know you're here," she said, and spoke briefly into the phone. When she'd replaced the receiver, she asked him, "Is that a vintage tie?"

"It's from 1952."

She nodded. "I love the look you're working. Scruffy but polished. It's quite chic."

"Thank you," he said, and grinned appreciatively, even though he'd worked hard this morning not to look scruffy.

Soon Violet came through the inner door and introduced herself. She reminded him of people he knew who worked over at the library, relaxed and personable, her dark hair pulled back.

"I'll take you into the stacks," she said, "but first I should have a look at your credentials."

Mason was ready for that. He pretended to feel his breast pocket, then his pants, his eyes growing wide. "Christ, I don't even have a business card on me. I left my briefcase in my car. That was stupid."

Violet frowned, waiting for him to continue.

"Listen, isn't this stuff public record anyway? I just want to do a little preliminary digging."

"Technically, yes," she said. "But we need to know who you are."

Mason bit his lip, feigning deep thought. "I had to park all the way over at Pershing Square. It'll take me half an hour to walk there and back. Can I bring my card in after lunch?"

She hesitated, pursing her lips.

"I promise I won't break anything," he said, and flashed her a smile.

After a few seconds she nodded and said, "Come on back," leading him through the inner door. A couple of people sat working in cubicles. The lone office, glass-fronted and no bigger than the cubes, sat empty. As they walked by he saw the plaque beside its door:

VIOLET HERNÁNDEZ
CHIEF ARCHIVIST

Violet walked past the cubes and pulled open another door. The paper archive—row after row of tall shelves filled the cavernous space. A sweaty-looking guy sat in front of a computer screen at a desk just inside. He looked up at them, startled at the interruption.

"Brian, this is Mr. Braithwaite. He'll need your assistance in the stacks."

"OK," he said, looking Mason over suspiciously. "I haven't seen you here before."

"I'm new at this," Mason said, and smiled at him.

"I'll leave you to it," Violet said, and left.

Brian got out of his chair, seemingly with much effort, and walked over to the nearest rack of shelves.

"The records are organized by quadrant, and within those, by date," he said, intoning an oft-recited spiel. "If you need to get to the higher shelves, there's a ladder by my desk. The rules are, no refiling—leave whatever you pull on my desk—and no photocopies. We can make them for you and issue them officially by mail. Ask me for a request form if you need copies."

"Why by mail?" Mason asked, surveying the dusty old accordion folders crammed onto the shelves.

"Copies have to be officially stamped."

"OK. Why do they have to be officially stamped?"

"You haven't done much work with government, have you," Brian said, his eyes narrowing.

"I haven't."

"Well, whatever the reasons are, they're way above my pay grade. I just follow the rules."

"That sounds wise," Mason said, nodding and furrowing his brow. "Is there a map where I can figure out what quadrant I need?"

Brian frowned. "Don't you know that already?"

"I left my briefcase in the car."

"There's a grid map on the wall at the end of the second aisle," he said, pointing it out, and returned to his desk.

The map was taller than he was, a faded color print of the southern half of the state, overlaid with myriad tiny numbered squares. Stooping to peer at the wall, he found Penstock Canyon and its little zone. He wanted to write down the numbers for it, but he didn't have his notepad with him. He could ask Brian, but he didn't want to seem any less professional than he already did. Checking his pockets, he found a pen inside his jacket, and wrote the string of numbers on his palm.

It took him a while to figure out the filing system, walking slowly along the rows, hunting for the right numbers. Absorbed in his screen, Brian ignored him, even though he sat facing the room, every aisle in his line of sight.

When he found the files about Penstock Canyon, they amounted to less than half a shelf, just six accordion boxes. He pulled the first one out and flipped it open, breathing in the distinctive aroma of ancient paper. Some of the contents were stapled or clipped together, but most were loose pages. He sat between the shelves, spreading the pages around him on the carpet. Brian glanced up, curious but not concerned, and went back to his screen.

The folder contained mostly unintelligible numerical data, charts and tables, and the occasional illustration. Some of it was old, forms filled by hand in spidery script. It seemed to be about core samples, but he didn't have the scientific background to make sense of it. He looked through every page, reading and scanning, but none of it was informative.

The second folder was equally impenetrable, as was the third, with older documents interspersed with newer ones, not organized by date as Brian had promised. He was starting to lose hope, but the next folder had thicker bundles of documents, including a seismic survey from 1967 that for some reason had been written in straightforward language. It read less like a scientist's notes and more like a report prepared for someone, he realized.

The writer said the oil deposit below Penstock Canyon was "remarkably shallow," just sixty feet deep in places. "The condition of the mineral deposits was unknown until now," he explained, "and wasn't taken into consideration during urban development." From his earlier research Mason knew the neighborhoods around Baldwin Hills had been built out a decade before this report had been prepared, but he had no idea whether it would mean anything for a pending construction project. Surely even a massive condo building wouldn't need to dig that deep. But there was that word, *remarkably.*

With a little research he could probably figure out whether the new information had ever become widely known, whether it had impacted new construction after 1967, and whether it was actually even significant, but he'd need a copy of this document. Asking Brian for an official one was an option, but where would he tell him to mail it? His lies would start unraveling. What he really needed was to make his own copies with his phone. He couldn't hide that from Brian, but maybe he could find a way to be alone for a few minutes.

Going through the rest of the folder, he didn't find anything nearly as informative or tantalizing as the 1967 report. He recompiled it and slid it into the empty slot it had left on the shelf, ignoring that Brian had told him not to, then dug through the remaining pair of boxes, similarly in vain. That was the full extent of the mineral archives on Penstock Canyon, he thought, sliding the last folder into place. They hadn't been informative, except that one report. It was maybe forty pages long. He looked over at Brian, still absorbed in his screen, and pulled the fourth folder out a little, positioning it to hang slightly over the edge of the shelf, so he could find it again quickly.

He went over and stood in front of Brian's desk.

"I'm going for lunch," Mason said. "Will I be able to get back in here if you're out?"

"I lock up when I leave," Brian said, "but today I'm going to eat at my desk. I'll be here when you get back."

"Great," Mason said, smiling at him as he left.

In a pedestrian arcade not far away he knew there was a noodle stand with a vegan option, and he sat at the counter, slurping up soba and tofu and broth.

After he'd eaten he pulled out his phone and started to look for local pastry shops. The noodle chef gently interrupted him, gesturing to the small crowd that was gathering behind him. He'd forgotten about the wonderful world of office work—of course a food vendor with five seats would be overwhelmed at lunchtime in a busy business district. He rose and pulled his wad of cash from his pants pocket, then paid for his lunch, smiling apologetically. Standing nearby, he resumed the quest for pastries.

There were a couple of vegan options within a few minutes' walk, he learned, which meant the only dilemma was whether to get macarons or cupcakes. Brian seemed more like a cupcake kind of guy, he decided, and set off for the vegan bakery.

The clerk was delighted when he ordered a dozen.

"Most people just buy one," she explained. "Everyone's always dieting."

Mason hoped Brian wasn't one of them. A dozen cupcakes required quite a large pastry box—he had to carry it with both hands back to Fort Ronnie. At the entrance, one of the security guards opened it to check the contents, and whistled appreciatively.

"Someone's not on the paleo plan," he said.

"Take one, if you want," Mason said. "They're vegan."

"Are they gluten-free?"

"Nope, sorry."

"Oh, well. Thanks anyway," he said wistfully.

The receptionist was gone when he walked in, but the door into the other offices wasn't locked.

Violet's office and the cubicles were similarly abandoned. Next to Violet's office stood a little kitchen area with a fridge, a coffeemaker, and a microwave. He set the box of cupcakes on the counter and propped the lid open, glancing around to make sure he wasn't being observed.

Examining the selection, he wasn't sure which one to eat himself. He'd asked for a variety, and there was indeed a riot of color here—four kinds of chocolate, and others with strawberry slices or berries stuck in the frosting. Not the Windex-colored one with the yellow sprinkles, he decided. It had to be chocolate. That would really sell it.

Peeling the paper off the dark chocolate one, he took a big bite, then pulled open the door to the archives.

"Someone brought cupcakes," he said breathlessly, his mouth half full.

Brian looked up in surprise. "Seriously? Nobody ever does that. Violet is lactose-intolerant, and Vera's on keto."

"They're freaking amazing," Mason said. "If you want one, you should grab it now."

"You're not supposed to have food in here," Brian said.

Mason stuffed the rest of the little cake into his mouth held up his hands, waggling his fingers to demonstrate his innocence.

Brian sighed and got up, then stepped out into the office.

As soon as the door closed, Mason hurried over

to the shelves with the Penstock Canyon records and grabbed the protruding folder. Pulling out his phone, he sat on the floor with his back to the door and pulled out the document, setting it on the carpet. The lighting was too low not to use the flash, which slowed him down a little, but he worked his way through it methodically, holding the device steady above it, snapping an image of the page, and quickly flipping to the next.

Brian didn't return for some time, and Mason was able to finish his skulduggery, dropping his phone into his inner breast pocket and riffling the paperwork back in the folder. He wandered over to Brian's desk, wondering if there was any point in looking at files for other neighborhoods while he was here.

"Those really were amazing," Brian said, stepping back into the room, his eyes shining with the buzz of sugar. "I gave Vera one. She said they were the best she'd ever had."

"I thought Vera was keto," Mason said.

"I guess she's keto-flexible. Did you see the blue one? I can't figure out what flavor it was."

"Is blue not a flavor?"

Brian giggled like a toddler. "You must have had a dark chocolate one. There's still a little on your face."

"Thanks," Mason said, and wiped his lips. "I'm heading out now. I appreciate your help."

He frowned. "Don't you need any copies?"

Mason nodded. "I will at some point, but I need

to double-check with the eggheads at headquarters about the date range they need. I'm sure I'll be back."

Violet was still out, he saw as he went by, and only four cupcakes remained in the pastry box. The receptionist was at her desk, and Mason waved to her on his way out, saying, "See you soon."

On the train he scrolled through the images he'd taken, happy to find that every page was showing up legibly. Now he just had to figure out what it all meant.

■-■-■

The house was empty when he got in. He peeled off his suit and sniffed the armpits to decide whether it needed to go to the cleaner. It never did, amazingly, no matter how much he wore it, the sci-fi fabric somehow repelling his sweat. He put it back on its hanger in the closet, then stopped when he saw himself in the floor mirror. There was a big smear of chocolate frosting at one side of his mouth. He leaned closer to examine it, then wiped it off. He'd ridden all way home from Fort Ronnie like this. He was actually one of those odd people on the metro that he'd told Peggy about.

He looked at his body in the mirror, standing there in his underpants. Not bad, he thought, although he could probably cut back on the cupcakes. The *chaneques* had told him to talk to his reflection in the water by their camp. It had helped him a lot. He wondered if any mirror could do that, or if it only worked in their pond, in their realm. He gazed into his own eyes, remembering that night, the state of mind he'd been in.

"What do you think?" he asked his reflection.

His image didn't change, but he saw the realization dawn in his eyes. He could access it here—that other version of himself, whatever it had been—if he wanted to, if he just tuned in to it. He'd been in the hidden mind state for hours that night, deep inside it, and it only took a few minutes to induce it now, narrowing his eyes to slits and imagining his awareness dispersing around his head. Eventually he got tired of looking at his own face, and turned away.

But his reflection didn't.

He froze, then slowly turned back, looking at himself, examining the mirror. It still looked like him, but it wasn't his mirror image any longer.

"You look good in your skivvies," his reflection said, nodding approvingly. "Good, but not great."

"Uh … you too," Mason said.

"How did you know Boring Brian would get distracted by snack treats?"

"Everyone loves cupcakes," Mason said, staring at himself. "Who are you? Are you my subconscious?"

His reflection laughed and rubbed his nose with his palm. "Look in the mirror, chum."

"Chum?" That didn't sound like him. "That's not really an answer."

"Listen, while I've got you here, there's something we should talk about."

"What's that?" Mason asked, apprehensive. His reflection seemed a lot more candid than he was.

"Lay off Kevin."

"What?"

"He's helping Gilbert a lot. You can tell just by talking to Gilbert that he's in a better frame of mind."

"I didn't say anything to Kevin," Mason protested.

"It's your attitude. You think your judgments are just for you, but they affect people. Gilbert trusts your opinions. You don't think he does, but he takes you seriously."

"OK," he said. "I'm going to step away now."

His reflection raised one palm and said, "Ciao, baby. See you soon."

Out of view of the mirror, he tried to clear his mind. It was unsettling to interact with himself. He arched his back, stretching his arms. He was exhausted, he realized, after getting up so early. The bed looked inviting, so he crawled in, avoiding the mirror.

The reflection was something from his own mind, he thought, stretching out under the covers and appreciating the warmth. It didn't seem like an independent entity, even though it had felt different from him.

Maybe it was like the Ouija board, pulling information out of the user's subconscious. That was a comforting thought. A more terrifying possibility was that he'd somehow unleashed a distinct personality, or even his own id, allowing it to act on its own. But at least it was just in the mirror, not running around the streets. Whatever it was, it was too freaky to explore it further, he decided as he nodded off. Talking to himself in the mirror was a fast track to the psych ward.

It was dark outside when Ned woke him.

"Time for dinner," he said, sitting on the edge of the bed and gently shaking his arm. "Peggy made cashew cheese, so we're having quesadillas."

"Yay," he managed, his voice hoarse. "I'll be right out."

They'd made corn on the cob as well, and by the time he joined them, everything was on the table.

Mason ate his quesadilla with great enjoyment, savoring the cheese. "Do either of you know someone who could interpret an oil survey?" he asked them. "I have a seismic report on the oil field under Penstock Canyon from the 1960s."

"You need a geologist," Ned said.

"Matt knows a lot of science types at Cal State," Peggy said. "I'll ask him."

"Good idea—I can text him. There's a public hearing on Thursday, and that's probably my last chance to have any input on The Palms."

"So you managed to get into Fort Ronnie," Ned said, raising his eyebrows appreciatively over his corn.

"It's that suit," Mason said. "I put it on, and

people believe whatever I say." He told them how he'd bluffed his way in and managed to obtain the document. Ned laughed at the cupcake story, shaking his head.

"I'm glad you're not really a lawyer," Peggy said.

After they'd eaten, he went into the office and pulled out his phone, texting Matt to ask if he knew a geologist, then sent a text to Gilbert.

> Glad things are going well with Kevin. It seems
> like he's helping you a lot.

Kevin might be interested to hear about his visit from the man in the mirrored sunglasses, he thought, staring at his phone. But he didn't feel the need to tell him. The visitor had come to talk to Mason—Kevin could take care of himself.

He spent some time organizing the photos he'd taken of the seismic report, then printed them out. It was so satisfying to hold it in his hands, this potentially significant replica, liberated from the bureaucrats at Fort Ronnie.

TEN

The ringing telephone woke him in the morning. He rolled over, scrabbled for the device, and saw that it was Matt.

He cleared his throat. "Braithwaite."

"Oh, fuck—I woke you."

"No, no, I'm up," Mason said.

"It seems to happen no matter what time of day I call you."

"Dude—it's fine. What have you got?"

"You said you needed a petroleum geologist, stat. A friend of mine does that in the private sector. Her name is Dolores. Have you got a pen?"

Mason grabbed his bedside notepad and scribbled down the number. "I appreciate this."

"No worries. It's just an intro. She'll be expecting

your call."

He rolled out of bed, shocked awake by the cold air, and pulled on his clothes, then went to the kitchen to make coffee. Once he was sufficiently lucid, he called Dolores.

"You're Matt's friend," she said, after he'd introduced himself.

"I have a seismic survey report that I'd like to have interpreted. Is that something you can do?"

"It depends on what kind of data you have," she said. "Can you email it to me?"

"It's actually from the 1960s, so it's on paper." He could email her the images of it, of course, but he wasn't going to share something he wasn't supposed to have with someone he'd never met.

"Well, maybe you could bring it over. I work in Westwood. Do you want to come for lunch?"

"Have you been to that vegan burger place by the theater?" he asked.

"I love that place," she said. "Let's meet there. How will I recognize you?"

"I'm fairly tall, and I've got extremely red hair."

Mason hustled to get ready. Decent public transit was sparse on the Westside, so he'd have some pedaling to do from the train. He stuffed the seismic report into his backpack, then coasted down the hill to the metro, standing with his bicycle and changing trains. Pedaling the last few miles, he got a little sweaty despite the cool weather.

The burger joint wasn't that busy, and Dolores waved to him when he walked in. She was dressed casually for an office worker, he thought, in a polo shirt, but she wore her dark hair in a trendy short style. Mason introduced himself and sat across the table from her.

"I hope you weren't waiting," he said.

"I just got here. You're right on time, but you look like you had to run."

"I cycled from the train," Mason said, grinning. "It's uphill."

"Good for you," she said emphatically. "And brave. I'd be too afraid to ride around here with all these cars."

"It's not so bad if you take the back streets."

A waiter came by to hand them menus, but Dolores stopped him. "I already know what I want," she said, and ordered a salad.

Mason didn't need the menu either, and asked for coffee and a veggie burger with greens on the side.

"I went to school with Matt," she said, when the waiter left. "How do you know him?"

"That's a good question," he said, and looked away, not sure how much he should reveal.

"Is it some psychic thing? It's okay—he's out with me about that."

Mason smiled. "That's a relief. Yes, he's a colleague in the field. He's also dating my roommate."

"Oh, I've heard about her," she said, as the waiter set water glasses on their table. "You're the gay guys."

"One of them," he said, and dug in his pocket for his business card, handing it across to her.

"You actually work as a psychic," she said, scanning it. "Is the seismic survey related to a case?"

"It is."

Her expression became serious. "Let's see it."

He pulled the report out and handed it to her.

"Someone's been to Fort Ronnie," Dolores said, and spent several minutes flipping through the data and the author's comments. The waiter brought Mason's coffee, and he sipped at it while she read. Eventually their food arrived, and she set the document on the seat beside her while they ate.

"Why do you want this information analyzed?" she asked, looking at him and poking at her lettuce with her fork.

"I have a client who's concerned about a construction project on a chunk of land covered by that report. Do you know those faux-rabian palaces all over town?"

"Douglas Grankin," she said, meeting his eye. "I've heard about that guy."

"Right. He's building another one in Penstock Canyon."

"Has the EIR been done?"

"Not yet. There's a public hearing for it tomorrow." He bit into his burger, leaning over his plate so that the sauce wouldn't drip onto his lap.

"Submit this," she said, glancing down at the report. "It'll get their attention."

"What does it mean?" he asked.

"There's a pocket of oil right below the surface. It's not uncommon around here, but it's not safe to build a huge building on it either. A house, sure, but not a monstrosity like Grankin's palaces. The deposit is only sixty feet down, and it's huge."

"Will that information stop the project?"

She nodded. "Maybe. If not, it'll definitely slow it down."

"If I was able to get this, won't the people doing the EIR have it too?"

"Not necessarily. They're not obligated to track it down. They also might choose to disregard it, and not even include it in their findings."

"That seems so corrupt."

"That's not the word I'd use," she said, setting her fork on the table. "Regulators are responsive, not proactive. If your house burned down, regulators would install a hydrant on your block for next time. But they're not going to tell you beforehand to fireproof your house. Insurance companies care about that stuff, but the prime directive for regulators is not to get in the way of commerce."

Mason nodded. "I'll make sure it gets to the hearing."

"More than that, make sure it gets into the public record. Stand up and read part of it. That way no one can deny that they know about the oil deposit. Otherwise, it could just get filed in another folder somewhere." She picked up the report and flipped through it. "I'll highlight a salient paragraph or two."

"Thanks."

"I might also be able to get you some clearer

documentation about Penstock Canyon," she said, handing the report to him. "Can you come back to my office?"

"Of course," he said, and waved at the waiter for the check.

Out on the street, Mason wheeled his bike as they walked the few blocks to Dolores's office. It was a modest high-rise for the neighborhood, emblazoned with the corporate logo of Ladra Oil. From his reading he knew the company was a major player in local extraction—not a transnational conglomerate, but far larger in scale than the likes of Brigid Petroleum.

Upstairs, they passed a reception area and walked down a lifeless hallway with doors lining both sides. Hers was a cramped little space, with stacks of paper covering every surface.

"Sit," she said, waving to the chair in front of her desk. "Can I see the report?"

He handed it to her, then moved the file folders from her chair to the corner of her desk and sat down.

Dolores worked intently for half an hour or so, the printer on her credenza occasionally churning out a page or two. Mason sat quietly, reading his email on his phone. Finally she gathered the prints and spent a few minutes with a pair of scissors, cutting a thin strip off the end of each page.

"I don't want my employer's name to turn up in someone else's EIR," she explained, "so I'm taking off anything that identifies Ladra." She met his eye, and spoke quietly, even though the office door was closed. "The work I do here is considered proprietary information, so I really shouldn't be handing it out. But it's for a good cause."

"Are you an environmentalist? Is that why you're helping me?" he asked.

She laughed. "It's hard to make that claim, working here. But I agree with your client—the city doesn't need another overpriced condo mega-complex."

Finally she handed him a sheaf of papers—the seismic report with a few sections highlighted in yellow, and the trimmed printouts.

"I overlaid a map of Penstock Canyon with the seismic data," Dolores explained, pointing out one of the sheets. "It's a rough sketch, but it doesn't get much clearer than that."

The other pages included a couple of cross-sections of the land, showing the oil deposit as a big black bubble below the surface, and an extract of the relevant section of the California Environmental Quality Act.

"A properly done EIR would pull all this together," she said, "but if you take it to the committee as public input, it'll be much harder for them to ignore."

"This is great," Mason said, leafing through the pages. "It's the first glimmer of hope I've had on this case. I can't thank you enough."

She stood. "Ladra Oil's interests align with Grankin's. They'd fire me in an instant if they found out I was helping."

"I understand." He rose and arranged the

paperwork in his backpack.

"So whatever happens, you can't mention my name. All this stuff came to you from an anonymous source."

"Your name won't come up. You have my word," he said.

He thanked her again and made his way back to the street, where he unlocked his bicycle, straddling it on the sidewalk for a minute while he thought about what to do. Dolores's input was more than he could have hoped for. The logical thing to do was pass it on to Janice.

Pulling out his phone, he dialed her number, and was glad when she picked up.

"I found some stuff that you're going to want to see before the hearing," he said. "I think it's good news."

"Great. I'm at work now—can you swing by tonight?"

"I'll be changing trains downtown in an hour. Maybe we could meet near your office?"

"Sure—there's a coffeehouse between here and the metro at Seventh Street."

Riding back toward the station went faster because it was downhill, and he was buoyed from learning so much of value from Dolores. He couldn't stop smiling, feeling the rush of success.

In the financial district he locked up his wheels and found a print shop, where he made two sets of photocopies of everything Dolores had given him. He could feel the extra weight of all the paper in his backpack as he walked to the café to meet Janice. It was satisfying, that sensation, knowing it might be weighty enough to derail Grankin and his development.

Janice wasn't at the café when he arrived, so he ordered espresso and guacamole and chips. She found him munching happily a few minutes later.

"Don't get up," she said, waving impatiently and sitting across from him. She looked sharp, in a tan suit with gold jewelry, her hair neatly bundled behind her head.

"Guacamole?" he offered, even though there wasn't much left.

"I've eaten, thanks," she said, and ordered a coffee from the waitress. "So what did you find?"

Mason wiped his fingers and dug into his bag, handing her a set of copies. She started reading, going through the pages slowly and methodically. That must be the legal training, Mason thought, and went back to the guac.

After a few minutes, Janice looked up at him, grinning broadly. "This is brilliant, Mason. Where did it all come from?"

"About that," he said. "How problematic is it if I obtained some of it under false pretenses?"

She looked him in the eye. "Did you steal it?"

Mason shook his head. "I distorted the truth slightly to get access to the state archives. I made a copy, but it wasn't issued officially."

"Who cares?" she said, and reached for her coffee cup. "As long as you didn't remove the original. The hearing tomorrow isn't a court proceeding. It doesn't matter how you got it."

"The geologist who did those maps assures me it's irrefutable. It should be very bad news for The Palms."

"Who's the geologist?"

He sipped his espresso. "I can't say. She prepared this stuff using her company's software, which could get her in trouble."

"That, I can understand. I'm no geologist, but it looks pretty ominous to me. My house is right over this oil too." She looked back to the pages in her hand. "Can I keep a copy?"

"It's yours."

"I'll put it all up on the No Palaces website, but this really needs to be presented at the hearing. It's the best way to keep it from getting overlooked or buried."

"That's what she said."

"You should speak tomorrow, and get this on the record."

"Me? That's why I brought it to you."

"I can voice my own opposition as a neighbor, but I can't go in there with anything this official-looking. My firm reps lots of real estate and development firms. It would be a conflict of interest."

"Someone else in No Palaces, then."

"The group isn't organized enough to take this on." She set the papers on the table.

"Maybe I could call one of the members and brief them on all this. It's pretty straightforward."

She sighed. "OK, Mason, full disclosure: there is no one else. I'm the only person in No Palaces."

"Seriously?"

"It's not that big a deal to speak at a hearing. There won't be anybody there but officials. You already know the material, and you're the one who spoke to the geologist."

"It sounds terrifying," he said, frowning.

"It's not. Plus, you know it's the right thing to do."

He sighed. "I guess it's inevitable, then."

She pulled her phone out of her jacket pocket. "I'll get the address and time," she said, and tapped at the device, then held it to her ear.

"I already got the details last week," he said.

"You have to check the day before. They usually move it up and change the room a few days ahead."

"Why would they do that?"

"If you ask them, it's to sort out last-minute scheduling conflicts. If you ask me, it's to minimize participation." She held up her finger and spoke into the phone, asking about the hearing.

She repeated the location and the time aloud, eyeing Mason. He pulled out his phone and checked his calendar.

"It's an hour earlier, and in a different building," he said, typing in the new details. "I'm so glad you knew to double-check."

She shrugged. "It's part of my job."

"What else do I need to know?" Mason asked, pulling out his notepad.

"Public comments are limited to three minutes, so you have to be organized and speak quickly," Janice said. "You have to sign up on a sheet when you arrive, before the proceedings start, or they won't let you talk. Don't submit the paperwork until you're called to speak, and hand it to the chair of the committee. We can sit together, but it shouldn't look like we're collaborating. We can talk, but not too much. The last thing we need is for Grankin's people to think I've passed you this material."

"You said no one would be there," Mason said, frowning and looking up from his notes.

"No one will. Just a couple of the developer's people, a couple of us, and the commissioners."

"Fine," he said. "I guess I've got some homework to do."

He pulled out some cash for the check, then pulled on his backpack. Janice put a firm hand on his shoulder as they walked out.

"You're doing the right thing," she said firmly. "It's going to go really well."

"Thanks," he said, and watched her walk up the street. He knew she'd meant to be reassuring, but it sounded like what she'd tell a witness right before a trial.

■-■-■

Over dinner, he told Ned about meeting Dolores, and Janice, and the speech he'd have to make.

"This is such great news," Ned said. "You cracked it."

"It's possible. We'll have to see how seriously the regulators take it."

"You really should do more than just talk to the bureaucrats. Send it to Danny Santos."

It was a great idea. Santos was a friend, a journalist who worked at the weekly paper *Va-Voom*. Getting the media involved might help stir up opposition to The Palms beyond what Mason and Janice could do alone.

The first priority, though, was working on what he was going to say tomorrow. There was a lot to cram into three minutes. He typed up a list of the key points and ran through it a couple times, timing himself as he spoke, then worked on cutting it down.

With Ned's scanner he made digital copies of all the pages Dolores had prepared. He attached a copy of the seismic report and sent it all in an email to Danny Santos.

> I'm presenting the attached material at an EIR hearing tomorrow. It looks to me like Douglas Grankin needs to back off on his plans to bring gentrification and displacement to Penstock Canyon, or he'll put public safety and the environment at risk. I hope *Va-Voom* will hold him accountable if the bureaucrats won't.
>
> This is an exclusive, by the way—let me know soon if you're not going to write about it, so I can pass it along to other media outlets.

He knew gentrification wasn't really the issue, but he hoped that and the other keywords would get the paper's attention. He added a few notes about what Betty Lewis had told him about the neighborhood, and a link to find the plot of land on a mapping website.

Climbing into bed, Ned moved close to him, nuzzling his neck.

"I'm proud of you, speaking up for what's right."

"Aw." Mason turned and kissed him on the forehead. "I just hope I don't look stupid. Although that ship has probably sailed."

Ned chuckled. "I'm guessing there'll only be a few people there."

"Janice said that too. I guess what's really important is that what I say will have some impact."

"Wear the suit," he said. "They'll take you more seriously."

All the writing he'd done came back in the dream world, letters swirling around in front of him, jumping sideways when he tried to read them, fading behind others. Some were underlined in red, strobing angrily, throbbing like a skin infection. He managed to pull himself out of it, and lay awake for a few minutes, feeling queasy, so as not to tumble back in.

ELEVEN

Anxiety about his impending performance woke Mason early, and he sat in the kitchen for a few minutes, caffeinating and munching on fruit, before he went into the office.

"You're up early," Ned said, glancing up from his screen.

"Nerves," Mason said, and pulled up the speaking notes he'd made. Running through them again in his head, he was satisfied with the content and the brevity, so he printed the list and cut it into manageable slices, numbering each little page. He practiced reading it through a few times, standing in front of the floor mirror in the bedroom, wary at first, concerned that his disconnected reflection might appear. But it was something that had to be induced, he reminded himself. Happily it couldn't will itself into existence.

Eventually he felt confident that he could do a decent job. He put copies of the documentation into his backpack, along with his speech notes, then went out onto the balcony to get some air and clear his head before he had to leave.

Standing at the railing, looking at the hills, his thoughts flitted through all the possible scenarios where things might go wrong. He could trip and fall flat on his face. He could drop his notes and spend two of his three minutes collecting them again. It was just like Peggy's dream, he realized, where Mason was struggling to give the weather report. His current sense of dread came from anticipating the same kinds of obstacles she'd described. Hopefully no spiders or tangled wires would slow him down today.

He put on the suit, which still looked freshly pressed, and pulled his backpack on. Ned wished him luck, and he headed to the metro. On the train he remembered to take the strap off his pant leg, tucking it into his pocket. That was a good sign, he thought. Maybe he wouldn't wind up looking like an idiot today.

It was a good thing he'd left early, because it took some time to find the right building, buried in the warren of bureaucracy that was the Civic Center. When he did find it, the doors were locked. He cupped his hands to the glass and peered in, but the lobby was deserted. Looking around the street, he managed to flag down a sheriff's deputy walking by.

"How do I get in?" he asked. "I have a meeting in there."

"Go into the building next door," the cop said, gesturing down the block. "Then go to the basement level and walk back through the tunnel."

It would be difficult to make the hearing any harder to find, he thought. Thursday afternoon in a practically unmarked building with locked doors. But sure enough, after he'd emptied his pockets for the metal detector and a deputy had waved a squealing wand over his crotch, determining that his belt buckle wasn't a security threat, he found the stairs to the basement and managed to get into the right building.

In the last few steps to the door of the hearing room, he breathed deeply through his nose, telling himself to be calm. The predictions of an empty room turned out to be accurate—besides the three officials at the front of the room, there were only six or eight other people, including Janice. Most of them looked like bureaucrats rather than concerned representatives of the citizenry, although two men standing at the back stared at him openly from the moment he stepped in. Only Grankin's flunkies would be that interested in him, he decided, and he wasn't about to let himself be intimidated, and tuned them out.

At the table up front, with the commissioners sitting behind it, he found the clipboard titled LIST

OF SPEAKERS and added his name. So far there was only one other, John Smith. That sounded so fake, it had to be legit. When he returned the clipboard to the table, the official sitting closest shot him an annoyed look and reached for it, squinting as if reading what he'd written was giving him eyestrain. Mason smiled as he walked away, knowing the guy's attitude was for show.

Janice was on the left side, in the front row. He sat beside her and tucked his backpack under the chair. He didn't say anything to her, minding her request that they not be seen as together.

"Don't you look sharp," she said quietly, not looking at him, not leaning closer.

"I thought I'd be taken more seriously wearing a necktie."

"With these chimps, that's a good instinct."

Mason stifled a laugh.

"Are you nervous?"

"Of course," he said, keeping his eyes on the bored-looking commissioners. "Your name's not on the speakers list."

"What you're going to present eclipses anything I could say as a NIMBY neighbor," she said.

"Listen, last night I sent the whole packet of documents to a guy I know at *Va-Voom*. I don't see him here, but maybe he'll write about it."

"Good thinking," she said. "*Va-Voom* loves this kind of thing."

While they waited for the meeting to start, Mason spent a few minutes with his eyes closed, clearing his mind and calming down. He remembered Matt's energy node technique—it might help him now. It didn't take long to find the strongest local point, in the floor near the back of the room. He focused on connecting with it, picturing it in his mind, mentally plugging in to its power. It seemed to be calming him down, he thought, helping him slow his racing thoughts and pounding heart.

The commissioner in the middle spoke over the quiet conversations in the room. "I'd like to call this meeting to order."

"That's the chair," Janice said. "When you go up, give the report to him."

In preparation Mason pulled the fat sheaf out of his backpack, and tucked his speech notes into his breast pocket. They listened as the chair introduced himself and the other commissioners, and then outlined the process of environmental review, which Mason had already read about. Janice had certainly heard it before, and sat fidgeting impatiently.

Finally the commissioner who'd squinted at his writing consulted the clipboard and said, "The first speaker on the roster for public comment is John Smith."

One of the suits who had been so interested in him earlier walked up to the microphone.

"My name is John Smith," he said. "As a private citizen, I am overjoyed that such exciting new projects are happening in our city." He looked at everyone in the room in turn, making earnest eye contact, not using notes.

"He's one of Grankin's people," Janice said under her breath. "Has to be. Who else would say that?"

Mason murmured assent, and they listened to Smith's three minutes extolling the virtues of the megaproject. He was an ordinary-looking guy, but Mason disliked something about him, his preachy tone, or his obnoxious too-long red necktie, hanging down to his belt. Of course it was his words that were distasteful, not the man himself, but Mason struggled to keep his expression neutral.

"In summary, I look forward to a glorious future with this appropriate and insightful collection of homes."

Two of the attendees clapped loudly as Smith stepped away. The board chair spoke again.

"Next on the roster is … uh … Mason Bratwurst."

Janice surreptitiously elbowed him, as if there was a chance that Mason hadn't recognized the mangled rendering of his own name. He stood and carried the papers to the front table, handing them to the chair. The man looked up at him but didn't take the documents, so Mason set them down in front of him.

"Mr. Chairman," he said, and stepped toward the mic.

"That's not how you address me," the chair said, frowning at him over his glasses.

"Forgive me, your majesty," he said loudly.

The chair's eyebrows shot up. Mason cleared his throat and leaned into the mic.

"My name is Mason Braithwaite," he said,

enunciating his surname slowly and eyeing the chair, who wasn't paying any attention, instead flipping through the report Mason had given him. Looking around the room, Mason saw there was a camera set up at the back, pointed right at the mic. How had he missed that before? He felt his face redden, and struggled to keep his nerves in check. The node, he remembered. It was there in his mind still, and thinking about it helped him focus. He pulled his notes out of his pocket and found the first point.

"Anticipating the Environmental Impact Report," he began, moving back from the mic a little to reduce the volume, "I obtained a series of documents from the state land bureau and from oil company records—dating as far back as 1967, but with contemporary exposition—that shows the oil table is only sixty feet below the Penstock Canyon parcel where The Palms is supposed to be built. I've submitted a copy of these documents to the committee, and anyone else can find them on the No Palaces website. We've also distributed them to several local media outlets."

He glanced at his notes occasionally, soon forgetting his anxiety and speaking forcefully, growing more confident as he laid out his argument. He was on his last point when the chair called "Time."

"The people have spoken," Mason said, leaning into the mic for maximum volume. He raised his fist in the air and headed back to his seat. Janice and two other people he didn't recognize clapped wildly.

Taking his chair, he felt the relief washing over

him, his muscles relaxing. But they weren't done with him.

The chair glared at him, furious. "How were these documents obtained?" he demanded. "They're not properly stamped. There are procedures for procuring official documents, and procedures for filing them with this committee. My inclination is to reject this submission."

Mason stood and spoke as loudly as he could, hoping the mic would pick up his words for the written record.

"You don't have to accept it, if it doesn't conform to your rules," he said. "But you should read it anyway. *Va-Voom* and several other media outlets have happily accepted copies of it, so it's going to be in the news whether you choose to ignore it or not."

He sat down again, and Janice clapped him on the back. The chair knew he was stymied, and moved on.

"Next on the roster is a representative of the community group Decent Homes for LA," he said, reading from the clipboard.

The other beady-eyed suit from the back of the room stepped up to the mic. It quickly became clear he was also an ardent supporter of the project.

"Decent Homes for LA believes that this project will reduce greenhouse gas emissions in our city. It will also help protect endangered wildfowl and preserve wetlands."

"How is all that possible?" Mason asked under his breath.

"It's not. It's an Astroturf group," Janice said.

"What does that mean?"

"A fake grassroots organization set up by industry. In this case, Grankin and his cronies. Look at him. That guy is totally a lawyer."

"Even I can see that," Mason said.

"What he's going to say will make your blood boil," Janice said. "You don't have to stay—I will. You've done your part."

"Thanks," he murmured. "Let's be in touch."

He grabbed his backpack and made his way quietly to the door. It felt great to be out of there—he was happy that he'd done it, and happy that it was over. There hadn't been any of the feared impediments either, like in Peggy's dream. When he reached the top of the stairs and was about to head down, he saw John Smith come out of the hearing room. It wasn't strange that he was leaving too, but he was staring at Mason.

If this was the only way out, of course the guy would follow him. In his gut he suspected he might be up to something more sinister, but he brushed it off and trotted down the stairs into the tunnel, then back up again into the building that actually had a working entrance. As he stepped out of the stairwell, he saw Smith half a flight below, his ugly red tie dangling, looking up at him intently.

That look—there was no mistaking it as innocuous. He wasn't following Mason to exchange pleasantries, or congratulate him on his speech, or get his number. That look was sheer malice. What the hell was he up to?

Heart pounding, Mason considered what to do. He walked into the lobby and looked back toward the stairwell: Smith was still behind him, meeting his gaze with a determined sneer. His instinct was to run. *Think, Mason. Keep your sangfroid.*

He strode over to the pair of county cops at the entrance and put on a big smile. "How are you guys doing? Traffic slowing down?"

"Not much happens after three," the burly one said. "What can I do for you?"

"I'm concerned for my safety. This guy," Mason said, gesturing to Smith, who had stopped, loitering halfway from the stairwell, "has been following me. He spoke at a meeting I was in and called himself John Smith. Does that sound made up to you?"

The deputy's eyes narrowed, and he put his hands on his hips. "Sir?" he said tentatively, jutting his chin toward Smith, who had pulled out his phone, pretending to be absorbed in it and unaware of the cop. He turned away toward the stairwell and ducked back in.

The deputy shrugged. "I guess he didn't really want to talk to you."

"Not in front of a cop, obviously."

"Well, hopefully that'll be the end of it."

"I wish you'd go after him," Mason said, gesturing toward the stairwell.

"There's no point—I didn't see him do anything." He looked Mason over, his gaze not unsympathetic. "Listen—this is the only public exit. I'll stop him if he tries to leave in the next few minutes. That'll give you a head start."

"Thanks," Mason said, and waved to him as went out to the street.

If Smith was one of Grankin's thugs, it didn't really matter whether Mason avoided him now—if they wanted to mess with him, they knew where he lived. It was an unsettling thought. He wondered if he should warn Ned. He glanced back repeatedly as he made his way toward the metro station, but Smith was nowhere to be seen.

Passing a little coffee place with mirrored windows, he ducked inside. It was almost empty, so late in the day, dusk already encroaching. He ordered a double espresso and then summoned a ride-share on his phone. It probably wasn't much safer than riding the train, but he'd feel less exposed.

The car pulled up, and Mason carried his coffee out to the curb, scanning up and down the sidewalk, relieved not to see Smith.

Ned was in the kitchen, apron on, working happily, when Mason got home.

"How did it go?" he asked.

"Great, I think," Mason said, pulling off his backpack. "I'll tell you all about it after I change."

"Gilbert's coming for dinner," Ned called after him.

"With Kevin?" he asked, turning back.

"Kevin's leaving today. Gilbert's dropping him at

Burbank Airport on the way here."

The suit was still fresh and odor-free, despite all his sweating, and he hung it in the closet. He looked at himself askance in the bedroom mirror, not willing to indulge his reflected persona, even though it would be nice to talk frankly to someone, since he'd decided not to tell Ned or Peggy about Smith and get them all freaked out.

It didn't make sense to live in fear, he told himself. If Grankin wanted to send someone after him, he'd deal with it then. All he could do was keep the door locked and watch his back. That was probably the point, he realized. Smith's face had said exactly that: "Watch your back." A bully's power lay in psychological intimidation—they wanted to unnerve him, not necessarily do any physical harm.

Peggy got home soon after, and then Gilbert arrived. They sat around the dining table, and Ned set out a platter of neatly rolled crepes, oozing with spinach and cheese stuffing.

"Beautiful presentation," Peggy said appreciatively, moving a crepe to her plate.

"This is the best vegan crepe I've ever had," Gilbert said through a mouthful of food, gesturing with his fork.

"I bet it's the first one you've ever had," Ned said.

Gilbert covered his mouth, heaving with mirth. "That's true, but it's still really good."

"So Kevin went home?" Mason asked, cutting into his own crepe.

"I'm going to miss him," Gilbert said.

"How did it go sharing a bed with him?" Peggy asked. "He's a big guy."

"It was great. The grays only came once while he was there, but he helped me figure it out."

"How did he manage that?" Ned asked.

"He explained what they were doing, and helped me keep calm while it was happening. Once I figured out how to let go of the fear, it wasn't such a bad experience."

"So—what are they doing?" Peggy asked.

"That's way too personal, woman," he said, grinning at her and setting down his fork. "It's only for me." Serious again, he sat forward. "It's also not completely clear yet. But I realize now that I'm lucky to be having these experiences."

"You seem so much more grounded," Ned said. "It seems like Kevin helped you a lot."

"I have to thank Mason for finding him," Gilbert said.

"You knew you needed help," Mason said, "and you reached out. So it's really your own doing."

"I'm glad you haven't had any more involvement with them," Gilbert said. "The visitors, I mean. Kevin was worried about that."

Mason exchanged a quick glance with Peggy. He considered telling Gilbert about the visitor in the sunglasses, but decided to focus on Gilbert's turn for the better. Mason's involvement with the visitors was finished, he knew that instinctively, so he'd keep that story to himself.

Gilbert talked animatedly about Kevin, describing the weird toothpaste he used, laughing about how much soda he drank, how he always wore an undershirt. Ned cleared their plates and set out a bowl of pomegranate seeds and orange slices.

"So I hear you're a tax scofflaw," Gilbert said, turning to Mason.

Mason shot Ned a look. "You are such a gossip."

"It's not gossip if it's true," Ned said, shrugging.

Mason told Gilbert his theory about Grankin's harassment, and then told them about speaking against The Palms at the hearing downtown.

"Were you happy with the way you presented it?" Ned asked, spooning more pomegranate seeds into his bowl.

"I think so. I didn't trip and fall, at least, and I said everything I had to say." He turned to Peggy. "I couldn't help but remember your dream. I wasn't doing a weather report, and there was no confetti, but the feeling was similar, anticipating it beforehand."

"That's so interesting," she said, looking thoughtful. "I was sure it represented a real event, but it was just the emotional content. I guess I'll leave the prophecy to my homeboys."

"Prophecy isn't really how things work," Mason said.

Peggy raised her eyebrows. "So how do things really work?"

"Well, any prediction is based on linear time. But that's an extremely limited idea that we have because of the way we experience the world."

"What the hell does that mean?" Gilbert asked, frowning over his bowl of fruit.

"It means that no one can predict the future."

Ned stared at him. "But that's what you do for a living."

"Not predicting the future. I tease out connections in the wider universe, things that are hidden—I get insights. But I don't know what's going to happen tomorrow."

Ned laughed and sat back in his chair. "I swear I'll never understand you, Mason."

"But you love me anyway."

"Inexplicably, yes, I do."

TWELVE

A couple of weeks later, sitting on the balcony with his laptop on a warm afternoon, Mason finally got news about The Palms. Danny Santos had acknowledged receiving all the paperwork, but hadn't said whether he'd write about it for *Va-Voom* or not, promising only "I'll look into this." Mason had monitored the news, and checked in with Janice. He'd even invested in a lengthy and unfruitful phone session with the county development agency, hoping to find out when the EIR would be completed, or if any additional permits had been issued for The Palms.

But there had been no updates until now, in a brief email from Janice:

Congratulations to us. Check this out.

Mason clicked on the link, and a video from a local station's news desk came up. The little clock in the corner of the video frame showed that it had been broadcast a few hours ago. A photo of a faux-rabian palace floated above the shoulder of the intensely coiffed anchor, her eyes wide to project sincerity as she presented the story.

"The preliminary Environmental Impact Report on Douglas Grankin's The Palms condo complex, planned for Penstock Canyon, was released today, and it's not good news for the prolific developer. Documents obtained by *Va-Voom Los Angeles* and shared with us here at LA's number-one mega news source imply that the project is effectively doomed. The environmental impact mitigation measures laid out in today's report would be far too costly to implement."

"Yes!" Mason shouted. With a big grin on his face, he wrote back to Janice:

I'm so glad to hear this. No more palaces!

He spent the afternoon reading through the text of the EIR, and the article in *Va-Voom*. Danny had waited to cover the story until after the environmental report was out, but it didn't really matter: Grankin wasn't going to be able to build on the *chaneques'* land. He smiled again as he reread the story.

As the sun went down, it started to cool off, so Mason went inside to the office. It was almost dusk when he heard a sharp *snap* at the window. He looked up and heard it again. He stood and looked out at the little patch of yard and the street beyond. No one was out there, but it happened again, *snap!* He saw a pebble bounce off the glass. Sliding open the window, he stood and listened, but there was only the background rumble of the city.

"Can't you see me?"

He knew that voice. "Rowan?"

"I'm over here."

Mason looked where the voice seemed to be, but couldn't see anything.

"Give me a minute," he said. He had to shift into hidden mind. Narrowing his eyes, he worked to clear his head, disperse his consciousness. Rowan must have known what he was doing, because he could hear the little guy patiently humming a tune while he waited.

Eventually Mason could feel that he'd shifted his state of mind. And there was Rowan, standing on his single leg at the edge of the street, materialized in his line of sight.

"I can see you now," Mason said softly.

"Good. Heather wants to meet. Come with us."

"I can only see you."

"It *is* just me. I'm using the figurative 'we.' Get your butt out here."

In his altered state he felt no trepidation about following Rowan, and went to the front door, closing it behind him. He didn't bother to grab a jacket, thinking only about seeing the little man again, hoping he wouldn't break focus and lose sight of him.

But Rowan was still outside, waiting in the same spot.

"Why do they always send you?" Mason asked. "I'd think you'd get a pass because of your disability."

"This way," Rowan said, scowling and ignoring the question. He crossed the street, stepping into the foliage. Mason knew it was only a few feet deep, a little barrier of greenery before they'd emerge onto the neighbor's lawn, but that wasn't what happened. He followed as Rowan hopped and swung nimbly through the forest, which became denser and greener in the fading light. After a few minutes of Mason hustling to keep up, they emerged into the *chaneques'* familiar clearing, with the pond at one side and the fire blazing in the middle, tepees all around.

The little people were unconcerned about him this time, not bothering to hide but staring openly at the giant striding into their camp. A dozen of them were gathered around the fire. He recognized many of the faces from his first visit.

Sour Alan slipped from his perch on a log and looked up at him with a crooked smile. "I never thought you'd do it."

It wasn't really a compliment, but he seemed sincere. "Thanks," Mason said.

Heather got to her feet, standing on a log. "It seems that you've saved our land," she said. "The palace won't be built."

Mason nodded. "That's my impression too."

She bowed quickly from the neck and said,

"Thank you for your hard work."

Rowan was beside Mason, standing on a log, and spoke under his breath. "She's our leader, and that's a very great honor. You should bow back."

Mason did so—inelegantly, as it wasn't something he made a habit of, lurching forward and bobbing his head—but it seemed to greatly please his hosts. Heather beamed, and Rowan jumped up and down, unable to contain his excitement.

"We always pay our debts," Heather said to him, and then shouted toward the tepees. "Rudd! Bring the sack."

The little redhead appeared momentarily, dragging a burlap bag on the ground behind him. When he'd wrangled it inside the ring of logs, he let go of it, panting heavily.

"Your payment, as agreed," Heather said, and pulled the sack open.

The glint of the coins inside was overwhelming, blindingly beautiful even in the flickering firelight. He was mesmerized, and sank to his knees to get closer to them.

"Go on," she said. "Fill your pockets."

It was a delight beyond his wildest fantasies even to be able to touch one of them, never mind taking fistfuls for himself. His heart soared, and he caressed the precious things, then scooped up a handful and dropped them into his pockets with his keys and his phone. He wished he had bigger pockets, or more of them.

"Don't get too greedy," Sour Alan muttered,

watching from a distance.

"That's completely sensible," Mason said, looking up at him. "I have to be able to walk home."

Heather chuckled. "If you're ready, Rudd will take you back."

"I don't know how to thank you for this," Mason said, getting to his feet and feeling his bulging pockets.

"It's fair payment for services rendered," Heather said. "No thanks needed."

"Will I see you again?" he asked, looking around at the others. He didn't know them very well, but felt wistful at the thought of leaving.

"I should think so," she said, nodding reassuringly. "We live nearby."

"Come on," Rudd said, and started for the edge of the clearing.

"I love you guys," Mason called to them, looking back as he followed Rudd to the forest. Heather laughed and waved, and even Sour Alan had a smile on his face. He knew it sounded silly, but he felt connected to them.

By the time they emerged on the street in front of the garage, Mason was winded from struggling to keep up with Rudd, dodging the tree trunks and low branches.

"Do you know where you are?" Rudd asked him.

"That's my house," he said, and gestured across the street.

Rudd nodded. "Farewell, then, fellow traveler," he said, and darted into the foliage.

Mason watched him go, panting and feeling dazed, the emotional intensity of the experience quickly fading. He resisted the urge to walk around to the neighbor's gate to look into the yard where Rudd should be right now. More important than that was all the weight in his pockets, making his pants sag.

In the office he pulled out two handfuls of the coins, dumping them on his desk, and then froze, looking at the jumble in dismay. This wasn't the irresistible glimmering gold he'd amassed a moment ago—these were dull and ordinary coins, marked with the image of an eagle clutching arrows and the label ONE DOLLAR. Somewhere between the *chaneques'* camp and his office, the coins had changed. More likely, they'd just looked different in their world. Either way, he'd been duped.

He spent a minute hauling out all the coins and stacking them in even piles. They were all the same dollar coin, not a speck of gold among them. There were forty-six in all. Sinking into his chair, he surveyed the stacks. He'd done a hell of a lot of work for forty-six bucks. That would barely cover his photocopying costs. Plus the cupcakes, he remembered. Those expenses alone added up to more than this.

Picking one up, he examined both sides. This one was old, inscribed 1861—that was a long time ago, the eve of the Civil War, and the coin didn't look age-worn at all. Maybe it would be worth more than the face value. He checked the others and found every one of them bore the same year. The engraved image above the date was a woman with a shield inscribed LIBERTY, holding a stake or a spear with a hat on it. The Phrygian cap, he realized—the same hat the *chaneques* had made him wear.

He heard the gentle rattle of the garage door opening, then closing again. Ned was home. He stacked the coins at the back of his desk drawer, keeping one to show Ned, and went to greet him at the door.

"Great news for both of us today," Ned said, setting down a couple of grocery bags and kissing Mason hello.

"Your mortgage is back on track."

"It is," he said, beaming. "I heard about The Palms on the radio. You did it, Mason."

"It seems that way. My client dropped by to pay me too." He held up the coin.

"A silver dollar?" Ned said. "You need to raise your rates."

"There's more than one."

"Who would pay you in coins, though?" he asked. "That's weird."

"They are weird," Mason agreed. "But I think there's more to it. The coins are old, so maybe they'll be worth more than the face value."

"How old?" Ned asked, slipping off his jacket.

"Nineteenth century."

"Coins were made of real silver back then." Ned took the coin and studied it. "It looks new."

"Let's weigh it," Mason said.

Ned followed him into the kitchen and pulled

out his food scale, setting the coin on it.

"It's not precise," Ned said, "but it looks like about three-quarters of an ounce."

Mason pulled out his phone and checked on the price of the metal. "If it's pure silver, it's worth about twenty dollars."

"Great," Ned said. "How many do you have?"

"Forty six. That means I got paid about … nine hundred bucks."

"At least," Ned said. "They might be worth even more as collectibles."

"I can live with that," Mason said, picking up the coin and flipping it over in his hand. "Shutting down The Palms benefits lots of people, so there's more to it than just the money. Plus I'd happily mess with Grankin for free."

Ned grinned. "Come and help me with the rest of the groceries, Mr. Palace-Buster."

"I'll get them," he said. "You go change."

"Thanks—they're in the trunk of the Crown Vic."

Mason set the coin on the counter and scooped up Ned's car keys.

Earning forty-six dollars had felt like he'd been ripped off, and even nine hundred was less than he would have charged the little people if they'd been ordinary clients with bank accounts. Walking out to the garage, he smiled thinking about how excited he'd been, how entranced, pulling the coins from that burlap sack. Maybe they'd knowingly fooled him, manipulating his emotions, but more likely he'd fooled himself, seeing what he wanted to see. He was lucky to get anything, considering who they were, so disconnected from Mason's world; it wouldn't have been surprising if they'd paid him in twigs and leaves. He hauled the grocery bags out of the trunk and closed the garage door.

"The coins are still beautiful, even in my world," he said aloud, looking up at the night sky.

—■—

Dinner preparations were underway, Ned working in the kitchen and Mason sprawled on the sofa, when Peggy got home. After she'd changed out of her work drag, she took a stool at the bar, chatting with Ned.

"This is a beauty," she said, picking up the coin. "Where did it come from?"

"Ask Mason," Ned said.

"Someone paid me with forty-six of those," Mason said. He got up from the sofa and sat with her.

"Who would do that?"

"It was the client who asked me to stop The Palms," he said, shooting her a knowing look. "The silver in it is worth way more than a dollar."

"Don't sell it for the metal," she said. "It's worth a lot more than that. This is in pristine condition."

"How do you know that?" he asked.

"She's a renaissance woman," Ned said, leaning on the counter.

"Get your computer," she said, and Mason

brought it from the coffee table and pulled it open, sliding it in front of her. She typed and peered at the screen, then twisted it back to face Mason.

"Look," she said. "In pristine condition it's worth twelve hundred bucks."

"For one coin?" Ned said, shocked.

"I guess I did get paid," Mason said.

Peggy pulled the laptop back and scanned the screen. "Can you see the mint mark? It's a tiny letter printed under the eagle."

Mason held the coin to the light and squinted at it. "It looks like there's an *S*."

"It was cast at the San Francisco Mint," she said. "That means it's worth more, closer to two grand."

"If they're all worth that much ..." Ned's voice trailed off.

"I really got paid," Mason said, hardly believing it.

"Keep in mind, those are retail auction prices," she said. "No dealer is going to pay that much."

"Still," Ned said.

"Just don't sell them all at once. That'll push the price down."

They chatted happily about how he might sell them, and Peggy went to her room to relax before dinner. Once they were alone, Ned leaned closer to him.

"Mason, you just made at least fifty grand, maybe a lot more."

"I did not see that coming."

"You could go in on the down payment for this house."

"I could," Mason said, reaching for his hand. "Maybe it's time."

"Do you think you're ready?"

"All these threads and patterns—everything I've been through has led me here. It must be right." He met Ned's gaze. "Ready or not."

Also from Dagmar Miura

The Mason Braithwaite Paranormal Mystery Series

In the previous books in the series, no one is ever quite sure whether psychic investigator Mason gets results with actual psychic power or his more mundane flatfooting, but the disheveled redhead manages to resolve some intractable mysteries.

mason.dagmarmiura.com

The Slater Ibáñez Books

Don't mess with the hothead—or he might just mess with you. Slater is only interested in two kinds of guys: the ones he wants to punch, and the ones he sleeps with. Things get interesting when they start to overlap.

slater.dagmarmiura.com

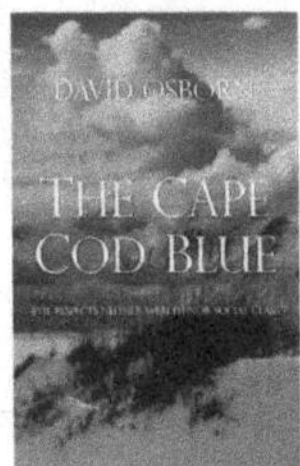

The Cape Cod Blue

The glittering, exalted world of art auctioning hides love, hate, and parricidal murder in a wealthy and socially prominent family when forgery of an anonymous Cape Cod painting is used to steal a world-famous portrait that's worth a fortune.

capecod.dagmarmiura.com

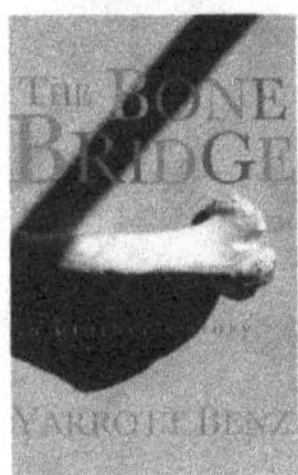

The Bone Bridge

Yarrott Benz, the 2016 Ippy Award winner for memoir, is forced to deal with extraordinary self-sacrifice in this harrowing account of teenage brothers, as different as night and day, trapped together in a dramatic medical dilemma.

bonebridge.dagmarmiura.com

9 781942 267508